The Abiding Image

The Abiding Image

Inspiration and Guidance for Beginning
Writers, Readers, and Teachers of Poetry

Cathy Smith Bowers

Press 53
Winston-Salem

Press 53, LLC
PO Box 30314
Winston-Salem, NC 27130

First Edition

A TOM LOMBARDO POETRY SELECTION

Author photo by Chris Bartol

Cover design by Christopher Forrest and Kevin Morgan Watson

Library of Congress Control Number
2020935140

Printed on acid-free paper
ISBN 978-1-950413-24-9

Contents

Invitation

The first time I taught poetry writing, I was just out of college, twenty-one years old, my hair hanging a little below the tops of my thighs. I had been assigned to teach senior English at Lancaster High School, the school from which I had graduated four years earlier. At that time in the South Carolina school system, the classes were divided into levels: the brightest students being assigned to level one classes; the mediocre students to level two; and all the rest, well, to level three. I, who had emerged from college imagining myself standing in front of a classroom pontificating the likes of Eliot, Pound, Bishop, Dickinson, and Yeats, was assigned five back-to-back classes of level threes. Several of my students were older than I was and the fewest I had in any of those classes was thirty. They were mostly male, rugged and rough young men who nodded throughout class, exhausted from having worked into the late-night hours, spinning and weaving and doffing in Springs Cotton Mill.

That first day I did something that these many years later I still consider one of the most brilliant pedagogical moves I have ever made. I announced to the students that we would be studying grammar, short stories, and novels. We would be writing short essays and brief research pieces. Then I got very quiet, affecting my most serious tone for my final decree—that if everyone worked hard all year, that if everyone conducted himself or herself as appropriately and respectfully as possible, then, and only then, would they be allowed to spend the entire last six weeks of school reading and writing poems. I would navigate the next eight months saying things like, "Only two more months until poetry time, guys!" Or, "Cut it out back there, you two, or both of you will be forfeiting your poetry privileges!"

I know now I was insane. But it was that insanity that got me through those first eight months of that first year of my teaching career. When the last six weeks of school arrived, after much reading and reciting of Dickinson, Hughes, Frost, Ferlinghetti, Brooks, and Hayden, we began writing our own poems—in class only—to accommodate those students who left after the final bell for their jobs in the mill.

I announced at the beginning of our writing week that I would choose the best poems written every day and *publish* them. That meant I would type the poems up and thumbtack them to the bulletin board at the back of the room. After all, I justified to myself, what did "publish" mean but "to make public"?

The day after the first batch of poems had been turned in, my students rushed into the room, flung their books on their desks, and elbowed their way to the back of the room to see who among them had been published. All week I watched this class-by-class storming of the bulletin board, naively assuming that by Friday each student would have produced at least a single image worthy of being displayed at the back of the room.

That first year, in my last class of the day, I had a student named Michael Viglioni. Michael was a bear of a boy, huge and gruff, one of the slowest of the slowest of these level threes. He stayed in trouble half the time. And as far as the writing of poetry, Michael could have been the butt of that old joke: "You know, Michael, there's no such thing as a bad poem; however, if there were, this would be it." It didn't seem to help that his very own name was a perfect line of trochaic trimeter: *Mi·*chael *Vig·*li·*on·*i.

Once, during a discussion of metaphor, I asked the students to create their own—to think of an object in nature and compare it to something very different but possessing similar character-istics. After a few minutes of scribbling and erasing and scribbling some more, hands began to go up. "Night is a robber!" someone shouted. "The snow is a shroud!" someone yelled. And then

Michael Viglioni, more animated than I had ever seen him: "The sun is a big flaming ball of fire in the sky!"

So, as the days of that final week dwindled, so did my hopes that Michael Viglioni's work would ever see the light of day—or at least the light of that auspicious bulletin board. My heart broke every day to see Michael Viglioni lumbering, crestfallen, back to his seat as the other students oohed and aahed over their posted poems glowing against the immaculate white of the paper I had so carefully typed them on.

But I was determined to adhere to my standards. After all, I was a first-year teacher, still holding to the pedagogical oaths to which I had sworn in my undergraduate Methods courses. Yes, only those poems that displayed—even in the most minute way— the elements of poetry we had been studying would earn a coveted place on the bulletin board. So, after the three o'clock bell rang on Thursday afternoon, I settled myself behind my desk to begin reading the day's poems when . . . dear God, Allah, Ganesh and all the saints included . . . there it was, a bright little jewel of a poem, brandishing, at the top of the page, none other than the name Michael Viglioni, written in all caps and finished off with a bold trinity of exclamation marks. I typed the poem in a feverish deluge of relief and happiness and pride, and next morning hurried to my classroom to thumbtack it right smack-dab in the middle of all the other poems now completely obscuring the bulletin board. Then it happened. I picked up the morning's listing of excused absences and in-school suspension casualties. Michael Viglioni's name was on the list. He would not be coming to class at all that day.

At Lancaster High School in 1972, study hall and in-school suspension were taught by the athletic coaches. Coach Danny Sawyer, the assistant football coach, was in charge of making sure the inmates of in-school suspension did not leave their designated cell at all during the day. Lunch would be delivered to Michael. And if Michael had to go to the bathroom, Coach Sawyer would lead him by the arm and stand outside the stall until Michael was ready to be escorted back to the desk at which he would finish out that day's sentence.

I bore the burden of my disappointment throughout the day until finally fifth period arrived. I had just gotten my class seated and settled down when I heard a loud knock at my door. I turned to behold through the glass top half of the door two huge visages that might have been those of not only the criminal, but the criminally insane. Coach Sawyer chewing his signature wad of Red Man tobacco and beside him, pressed to the glass, the pleading face of Michael Viglioni.

I stopped teaching and walked to the door. I opened it. Coach Sawyer's right hand held Michael's arm firmly in its grasp. "I'm really sorry, Miz Bowers, disturbing your class and all, but Michael here just won't shut up about needing to come over here to your room. Keeps saying something about a poem being published. I can't make heads nor tails out of what he's talking about. He knows he ain't supposed to leave that room to go nowhere but the bathroom but he—"

Before Coach Sawyer could finish his last sentence, Michael Viglioni had wrenched his arm free and was puffing and ambling his huge self to the back of the room toward the bulletin board as the rest of the class looked silently on. He stood there, eyes scanning for a few breathless moments all the poems typed up on fresh, crisp sheets of paper. And then he spotted it, his own little poem, solid and sure beneath his name—MICHAEL VIGLIONI—in all caps and complete with the exclamation marks I had typed over again and again to mimic the bold touch Michael had left on them. Then we watched in hushed amazement as he returned, head high and shoulders back, to the front of the class where he surrendered himself happily into the grasp of Coach Sawyer's custody.

That was several decades ago. Still, when I grow wearisome and unsure of the validity of what I'm spending my life doing, all I have to do is conjure up the face of Michael Viglioni, the only Michael Viglioni who will ever pass through this world. I know now why I put off teaching poetry until the last six weeks of school that year. Reading and writing poems was one of the things I loved most in the world, and I was terrified of offering the thing that had validated my life, only to have it rejected by what appeared to me on that very first day nothing more than a bunch of gangsters waiting for any opportunity to slit my throat.

Michael Viglioni's poem was not a great poem. It really wasn't even a good poem—at least not by the standards of most poets. But it was the best poem he could have written. I agree with poet and editor Alfred A. Poulin's belief that "the very act of writing poetry is an affirmative one, saying *no* to any force that would destroy the human spirit." And so, too, would the devoted poet and teacher Richard Hugo agree. For it is in his amazing little classic *The Triggering Town* that he compassionately asserts:

> What about the student who is not good? Who will never write much? It is possible for a good teacher to get from that student one poem or one story that far exceeds whatever hopes the student had. It may be of no importance to the world of high culture, but it may be very important to the student. It is a small thing, but it is also small and wrong to forget or ignore lives that can use a single microscopic moment of personal triumph.

In my own long career of writing poetry and teaching poetry writing, Michael Viglioni might have been my greatest triumph—the way he turned from the bulletin board that distant day, wearing, if only for a single moment, the face of a boy who had just entered the gates of paradise.

And so it is in honor of that abiding image that I dedicate this little book to Michael Viglioni, along with every other student I have had the great luck and pleasure to mentor. I also dedicate these lectures, essays, and vignettes to the aforementioned Richard Hugo, whose own slim volume, *The Triggering Town*, continues to nurture, instruct, and inspire me.

"I don't know why we do it," he says in his introductory pages. "We must be crazy. Welcome, fellow poet."

The Abiding Image

ONE

How to Read a Poem

When I was about ten years old, I began, to my mother's dismay, following my teenage brother and his friends around the neighborhood. One day I watched them watch Nancy Owens, an older girl in the neighborhood, round the corner at the top of Eleventh Street. "Slut!" one of the boys yelled out as she disappeared over the hill in the direction of Pete Byrd's grocery store. When I asked my brother what that word—*slut*—meant, he snickered and hemmed and hawed as the other boys jostled around him. Then he finally came out with something about girls *giving it up easy* and that if I didn't get on back home where I belonged he was going to teach me a few more words I'd never heard before.

Later, I asked my mother what it meant for a girl to give it up easy. When she finally regained composure, she responded in her usual wise and instructive way: "You shut your mouth, young lady, before I stomp the living daylights out of you!"

That was my sex talk.

It wasn't until I had been writing and reading poems seriously for many years that I finally understood the full meaning of "giving it up easy." Unfortunately, by that time, the good reputation my mother had so hoped and prayed for me was pretty much shot.

So, poems are like the 1950's *nice girls* my mother spoke so often and fondly of, in that the best ones don't give themselves up too easily, but yield slowly after having been courted with much patience, sensitivity, and care. But just how does one give a poem the proper reading it not only deserves but also requires for the reader to get beneath those delicate, often ephemeral, layers of compression and complexity? Let's begin by giving the poem at least four readings—the first reading for *feeling*, the second for *story*, the third for *language*, and the fourth for *line*.

FEELING

How many times have you been given this assignment by some well-meaning but—in my mind at least—misguided teacher: "Read the poem on page three thousand nine hundred ninety-nine of your literature book and write a paragraph explaining what it means." And how many times have you done just that—slogged your way through some poem deemed *great* by some invisible authority, a poem that hadn't yet moved you in any way that would make you even give a hoot about what all that mumbo jumbo might *mean*. But off you went with the designated poem, determined—as poet Billy Collins writes in his poem "Introduction to Poetry"—"to tie the poem to a chair with rope / and torture a confession out of it."

How much more open—and unintimidated—might you have been had the teacher made this assignment: "Read the poem on page three thousand nine hundred ninety-nine of your literature book and write down several adjectives describing how the poem made you feel."

I once heard poet Robert Bly say that when we read a poem silently from the page we take it into our heads but when we hear a poem, we take it into our hearts and into our bodies via our senses. The heart and the body are, indeed, the first places a poem should enter. This is how we *feel* the poem. Here is a powerful little poem by Nick Flynn from his collection *Some Ether*. Read this poem slowly, out loud if possible, letting the words and images wash over you. Do not worry about what the poem "means." There will be time for that later.

Bag of Mice

I dreamt your suicide note
was scrawled in pencil on a brown paperbag,
& in the bag were six baby mice. The bag
opened into darkness,
smoldering
from the top down. The mice,
huddled at the bottom, scurried the bag
across a shorn field. I stood over it
& as the burning reached each carbon letter
of what you'd written
your voice released into the night
like a song, & the mice
grew wilder.

How have these words and images and sounds left you feeling?
I can feel the roiling this poem has created inside of me: frantic,
anxious, dreadful, vulnerable, terrified, abandoned, desolate,
sad, alone. And angry. Very, very angry. Yet, for a moment,
toward the end of the poem, there is that brief sense of release.

Marion Stocking, previous editor of *Beloit Poetry Journal,*
speaks of "flawlessly work-shopped poems" that "fail to
ignite." When I come across a poem that ignites in me such a
powerful emotional response as Nick Flynn's "Bag of Mice," I
am ready and eager to look more closely at the poem. I am
ready now to think about *meaning,* or to get at what I prefer
to call the *story* of the poem.

STORY

Poet and editor Dave Smith says, "Some poems arrive with no
subject, consisting only of language. Often this is the language of
pretension or of raw matter, having all parts but one, like a laptop
computer without a hard drive but otherwise intact and shiny."
When a poem moves me in some way upon the first reading,

whether it is through sound, rhythm, a fresh phrase or image, I am compelled to read it again and again until I begin to discern the poem's story—or *subject,* as Smith puts it.

In high school I discovered the poems of Gerard Manley Hopkins, falling head-over-heels in love with pure sound. I would wander among the other students opening and clanging shut the doors of their lockers, quietly reciting "The Windhover":

> I caught this morning morning's minion, king-
> dom of daylight's dauphin, dapple-dawn-drawn
> Falcon, in his riding
> Of the rolling level underneath him steady air, . . .

Thank the gods and goddesses no one approached me to ask what it meant. My only response would have been—"Who cares!" But after several years of reciting Hopkins—simply for the feelings the sounds evoked in me—I did begin to wonder if those mesmerizingly beautiful words might also mean something. So I went to work—and hard work it was—looking up words in the *Oxford English Dictionary,* thumbing through thesauruses, researching and analyzing the connotations and denotations of all his lovely words. And, yes, Hopkins' poems do, indeed, have subjects—each a story imbued with layer upon layer of both literal and figurative meaning.

But back, now, to our own *subject* at hand—Nick Flynn's powerful little poem, "Bag of Mice." Now we are ready to read the poem again—this time for *story.*

Bag of Mice

> I dreamt your suicide note
> was scrawled in pencil on a brown paperbag,
> & in the bag were six baby mice. The bag
> opened into darkness,
> smoldering
> from the top down. The mice,

> huddled at the bottom, scurried the bag
> across a shorn field. I stood over it
> & as the burning reached each carbon letter
> of what you'd written
> your voice released into the night
> like a song, & the mice
> grew wilder.

An attempt to paraphrase can certainly help get us closer to the subject or story of the poem. We might begin by identifying the speaker and the occasion of the poem. The speaker of "Bag of Mice" seems to be someone telling about a dream he or she has had about another person's suicide note. Is the speaker male, female? Is the suicide victim male or female? Though further research into Nick Flynn's life reveals that his mother committed suicide, nothing in the poem itself suggests either the speaker's or the deceased's gender. And since the speaker of the poem is not necessarily the poet himself or herself, it's best to refer to the speaker as *the speaker*. Neither does the poem suggest who the writer of the note was or the writer's gender. We can say, though, that there is a speaker who has dreamt about a suicide note written on a brown paper bag. We can say the note was written in pencil. We can say there were six baby mice at the bottom of the bag. We can say the top of the bag was burning very slowly. We can say it was dark—at least at the bag's opening. We can say the bag was moving quickly across a field, propelled by the mice inside. We can say the field was cut very close to the earth. We can say the speaker watched everything, even the letters of the note as they burned one by one. We can say the author of the note's voice was set free by this burning. And we can say that upon the freeing of the "suicide's" voice, the mice, still inside the bag, became even more frantic and anxious and agitated.

This is pretty much all we can reasonably say at this point about the subject or story of the poem. But let's see if a third reading that focuses on the *language* of the poem can help elucidate even further what this poem is about.

LANGUAGE

Alexander Pope, in "An Essay On Criticism," says: "'Tis not enough no harshness gives offence / the sound must be an echo to the sense." Perhaps poet and editor Peter Cooley is echoing Pope's sentiment when he speaks of "submissions that are some kind of prose in drag." Each of these poets seems to give great import to the power of a poem's language not only to "echo" meaning but to illuminate it. A poet may use a number of literary tropes to illuminate a poem's subject, story, and larger meaning.

Here again is Nick Flynn's "Bag of Mice." Read it a third time paying attention to language: diction (word choice) that resonates on more than one level; sound; and tropes, such as simile, metaphor, hyperbole, irony, synecdoche and metonymy.

Bag of Mice

I dreamt your suicide note
was scrawled in pencil on a brown paperbag,
& in the bag were six baby mice. The bag
opened into darkness,
smoldering
from the top down. The mice,
huddled at the bottom, scurried the bag
across a shorn field. I stood over it
& as the burning reached each carbon letter
of what you'd written
your voice released into the night
like a song, & the mice
grew wilder.

Among the words that continue to haunt me because of their many different levels of meaning are *scrawled*, *baby*, *smoldering*, *huddled*, *scurried*, *shorn*, *carbon*, *like a song*, and *grew wilder*. These are words, too, that can help us identify the *tone* of the poem, or the author's attitude toward his subject matter:

Scrawled: quickly and carelessly written, thus done in a negligent, thoughtless manner.

Baby: not only are mice tiny creatures, what makes them even more vulnerable is the fact that they are baby mice, possibly so young they do not yet have hair to protect them from the elements.

Smoldering: this word suggests a very, very slow, torturous process. These baby mice—in my mind the ones left to deal with the devastating effects of the suicide—are going to suffer this act for a long, long time. This is also—importantly, I think—a word we use to suggest anger: *I was smoldering.*

Huddled: to gather closely together, perhaps for protection; a private meeting to discuss serious matters; in football, a gathering to receive instruction (Yet, who is there, now, to give these baby mice instruction?).

Scurried: this word creates a tremendous amount of tension in the poem. The verb *scurried* is traditionally an intransitive verb—a verb that has no object. Yet Flynn has used it here as a transitive verb, its object being the word *bag*. One of my definitions for tension is "the upsetting of the reader's expectations." And with the odd use of this verb, Flynn, has indeed upset the reader's expectations.

Shorn: cut down to the bare skin; deprived of one's power. I never see or hear this word without thinking of the many victims of the Holocaust whose heads were shorn when they arrived at the concentration camps. I also think of the ancient humiliating ritual of shearing the head of a woman accused of adultery or collaboration. If these baby mice ever do escape this "fire," there will be only a shorn field to greet them—no food, no shelter, no means, whatsoever, of protection.

Carbon: this word echoes the detail of the pencil scrawl in line two. Carbon, unlike ink, suggests something that is impermanent, something that can be easily erased. Carbon is also the single element common to all living matter. It is the last thing left when the essence of a living thing is burned away.

Released . . . like a song: The only simile used in the poem, the only two words that have pleasant, comforting connotations— and they are given to the author of this suicide note.

Grew wilder: the final words of the poem—this is the legacy that the deceased has bequeathed to those left behind, a burden they will, perhaps, carry with them until they, too, are nothing more than carbon.

Besides all of these powerful, carefully chosen words, note Flynn's artful wielding of sound, especially his use of alliteration: **suicide/scrawled/six/smoldering/scurried/shorn/stood/song**—echoed by the internal use of the consonant "s" sound (consonance): **mice/darkness/mice/across/voice/released/mice.** All those "s" sounds create, as we read the poem, the hissing sound made by the smoldering bag.

Flynn works just as artfully with assonance—the repetition of vowel sounds: **reached/each/released,** and also **nice/like/mice/wilder.** Two of the highest frequency vowel sounds in the English language are the long *i* sound and the long *e* sound. Flynn implodes the final lines of the poem with these sounds—sounds that can create the effect of excitement, intensity, speed, energy—in this case, an energy created by the desperate situation that has left these baby mice growing only *wilder.*

I find it interesting that Flynn's poem is almost free of literary tropes or figurative language. Yet, as I noted earlier, there is that one simile—**your voice / released into the night / like a song**—that is given to the writer of the suicide note. And since dreams communicate with us through metaphor, we are invited to ponder every aspect of the dream on the figurative level. Flynn's careful word choice, as we have seen, has given us a poem resonant with metaphorical implications.

Flynn's use of language creates and illuminates meaning, but what has Flynn done with the physical aspect of the poem to enhance meaning and create tone? This aspect of the poem is what I call *line*—the way the poet has put the poem on the page.

LINE

Laurence Perrine, in his classic *Sound and Sense: An Introduction to Poetry*, notes that pattern and form appeal "to the human instinct for design, the instinct that has prompted people, at various times, to tattoo and paint their bodies, to decorate their swords with beautiful and complex tracery, and to choose patterned fabric for their clothing, carpets, curtains, and wallpapers. The poet appeals to our love of the shapely."

So, just as we might be drawn to someone's arm or ankle flaunting a bright tattoo, so are we drawn to the way a poem looks on the page. The serious poet doesn't just "leave [the words] lay where Jesus flang 'em," to borrow a phrase from the delightful writer Anne Lamott. The serious poet considers line-length, stanza breaks, syllable count, line endings, enjambment, and—if the poem is written in form—metrics and rhyme scheme. But since Flynn's poem is written in free verse, let's pay attention to stanzas, line-length, word placement, and enjambments.

We need first to note that it is impossible to say what the poet intended as he or she was deciding how to put the poem on the page. Doing so would be committing that old literary faux pas known as the *intentional fallacy*. Consider all the ways Flynn's design illuminates or enhances, for the reader, feeling and story and language.

Bag of Mice

I dreamt your suicide note
was scrawled in pencil on a brown paperbag,
& in the bag were six baby mice. The bag
opened into darkness,
smoldering
from the top down. The mice,
huddled at the bottom, scurried the bag
across a shorn field. I stood over it
& as the burning reached each carbon letter

> of what you'd written
> your voice released into the night
> like a song, & the mice
> grew wilder.

The first thing I notice about the way the poem looks on the page is its jagged, chaotic right margin. If this poem could be lifted off the page and held in the hand, it might be used as a weapon—an instrument capable of inflicting pain, like the pain that has been and will continue to be inflicted on those left to deal with this ostensible suicide. The form is as chaotic as the frantic scurrying of those mice at the bottom of the slowly burning bag.

The second thing I notice is that the poem is a single stanza with only two brief pauses designated by commas at the ends of lines two and six. The entire poem of four sentences allows for four complete stops—but the only stop of these four that occurs at the end of a line is the final period. This strategy, known as enjambment, forces us from one line to the next as we read, as if the poem itself is *smoldering*—a slow, steady, unstoppable movement down the page.

It is also interesting that the word *bag* is used in the poem five times, and three of those times it has been given the most emphatic place in the line: the end. To me, this strategy forces me to pay attention to this word. And I think of yet another form of that word: *baggage,* a word used to refer to the emotional "stuff" we carry with us that often hinders the health and development and productivity of our lives. Will these baby mice, perhaps the children of the deceased, ever escape the bag or the baggage of this devastating act?

And what else are we asked to pay special attention to? Interesting that the only word given an entire line is the word *smoldering.* Could this strategy be a hint that we are to look at all levels of meaning of this word—including the connotation of *anger?*

I heard someone once say that the tone, or author's attitude, of "Bag of Mice" was acceptance and understanding of the need for release of someone who has committed suicide. I won't commit that old intentional fallacy I mentioned earlier, but I think I can safely guess—by the physical placement of the word *smoldering* and of the final phrase *the mice grew wilder*— that this is one more pissed-off poet. Or reader, at least.

Nick Flynn's poem "Bag of Mice" is a little poem that even on a single reading packs a huge emotional punch. And a reader who looks closely at what lies beneath its many layers will see that this is one poem that does not *give it up easy.*

TWO

The Abiding Image

The true mystery of the world
is in the visible, not the invisible.
—Oscar Wilde

When I first knew I was going to be a poet, I thought my task would be to come up with some profound idea, some deep truth only I was privy to, and then express that profound thought with the most impressive words I could think of—words with lots of syllables that would surely reveal to my readers just how smart I was. Perhaps, too, I thought, I should hide whatever it was I was trying to say so that my readers would have to work really hard to *get it*. After all, my teachers, time and time again, had instructed me to read some mysteriously obscure poem that he or she deemed *great* and to write a paragraph explaining what it meant. I quickly deduced, then, that for a poem to be great, it needed to be indecipherable.

So, in my first attempts at writing poems, I set out to dazzle my readers with a brilliant confusion of pithy abstractions. Much to my dismay, however, the profound ideas I had hoped to pour from my brain onto the long yellow pages of my legal pads never showed. I soon realized that not only did I have no profound ideas, I didn't even have any superficial ideas. I needed a new strategy: I would simply begin not with an idea but with an image that had been haunting me—sometimes for years, for decades—and I would, to the best of my ability, recreate in vivid, descriptive details everything I could remember about that image. Memory begets memory I soon learned. I also learned the wisdom of May Sarton's words: "[G]o deep enough and there is a bedrock of truth, however hard."

What a relief it was—releasing the notion that I had to *know* what it was I wanted to say before I sat down to write. In fact, I realized, if I already knew what it was I wanted say, why bother? For, indeed, hidden within the image—*the abiding image*, I soon came to call it—was Sarton's *truth,* the profound idea, the moment of insight. My job was simply to sit down with the abiding image and to describe, describe, describe. I would allow myself to write into the mystery of that abiding image. And what a delight to discover all that lay within what before had seemed only a random memory of an irrelevant moment in my life.

I read a few years back that the man who invented Velcro did it after studying closely the mechanics of *beggar lice*— what we in the South call those miniscule fruits of a variety of wild plants that stick to our shoe laces and hems of our jeans when we walk through an open field. What was it, he wondered, that made these things hang on so? Friction, the rub, the pulling against each other of opposites, that's what. That more-than-meets-the-eye thing. That thing that requires first a delving into the particular before we can get to the universal—i.e., those profound ideas I had hoped would simply appear in my brain without my having to do any of the hard work. Thank the gods and all the goddesses they never did. For had they appeared, I would have been deprived of the sense of discovery that is the true gift of the poetic process.

Why is it that what I remember most about my father are the tiny wisps of cotton that clung to his Adam's apple after a hard shift in the mill? Why is it that what I remember most about my brother Paul when he was dying of AIDS are the orchids he had begun growing, their bare and tendrilly roots relying on nothing more than air for their nourishment? And the house I grew up in—the rattle and clack of the window fan drowning out the Saturday morning voices of Popeye and Olive Oyl? My mother—the smell of her dark hair the night my father whispered into her ear the punch line of a joke my siblings and I were too young to hear? Why is it that what I remember most about September 11, 2001, is the okra I joyously dredged and fried for supper after learning my beloved older sister had not been on one of those planes?

I believe that life happens in metaphors. These images, vestiges of our waking lives, come to us through all five senses—touch, sight, sound, smell, and taste—and are as rich and as full of *deeper meaning* as are our nightly dreams. Each is a gift that holds within it a poem waiting to be birthed. And with the birthing of each poem, we, our selves, continue to be birthed, a little closer each time to the person we were intended to become.

After more than thirty years of writing poems and teaching the writing of poems, I still use a little exercise that helps me and my students call up the many abiding images longing to be explored. It's a silly little exercise, but as the late, great poet and teacher Richard Hugo says in *The Triggering Town*, "Poets are silly people." Perhaps the word *childlike* would be more accurate and less offensive to anyone still too caught up in ego to think of himself or herself as silly. It is, indeed, a silly, childlike exercise, but it never fails to work.

We begin by writing down five sentence stems to be fleshed out with concrete images—not ideas, remember—from our daily lives. Each stem contains the phrase *If my name were_____, it would be_____*. The first blank is filled in with one of the five senses, and the second blank is filled in with an image from our daily lives. It is amazing how quickly these images come, often images we have not thought about in years, decades even; images that long ago pushed themselves into the realm of the unconscious.

I have found that the first temptation with these images is to stop with the most obvious and to leave it at that. For example, if we are filling in the blanks thusly—*If my name were a color (sight) it would be blue like the sky*—we need to go back to the drawing board. First of all, this image is so generic anyone in the world could have come up with it. Poetry is about particulars, not generics. This is why I like to use the phrase *If my name were . . . .* The purpose of this strategy is to encourage us to look into the uniqueness of our own lives—those bits and pieces of ourselves that reveal the little spark of divinity many of us long ago forgot ever existed. It does, indeed, seem paradoxical that it's not our common experiences that draw us to each other, but the unique way each of us lived that experience. Here are some good examples of abiding images that came from a workshop I conducted several years ago:

> If my name were a taste, it would be the taste of quinine my mother covered my thumb with to keep me from sucking it each night when I was four.

> If my name were a texture (touch), it would be cold and sticky like the juice of the watermelon I devoured each summer on the old picnic table at my grandmother's farm.

> If my name were a smell, it would be the smell of fear in our house as my mother held me, her shoulder tensing under her cotton blouse as her eyes darted elsewhere.

> If my name were a smell it would be the scent of the pine-knot fire, nights of the foxhunts my father used to take me on.

> If my name were a sound it would be the sizzle each dawn of country ham frying on my grandmother's old black wood stove.

And finally, one of my own that I will continue to explore with you in the next chapter:

> If my name were a color it would be brown like the bags of groceries my boyfriend left on Mama's kitchen table every Friday night after my family broke up.

Now we have our abiding images, and we are ready to write into the mysteries of these images to perhaps discover why they have held onto us all these years. But before we start, please check all notions of profound ideas and impressive *poetic* language at the door. We must even check at the door the notion that we are about to write a poem. That thought in itself is enough to block even the most experienced poets. No, what we are going to do now is to sit down with our image and create what I call *a big old messy hunk of stone*. All we have to have is a little time, and a quiet place. But how in the world does one go about creating that big old messy hunk of stone?

Just follow me—it'll be fun!

THREE

That Messy Hunk of Stone

I love the legend of Michelangelo's creative process. Whenever he was about to create a sculpture—the *David* or the *Pietà*, for example—he would sit in front of his huge hunk of marble and study its surface until he could see the work of art that was already inside the stone. His job, then, was simply to chisel and carve away the wrapping of the *David* or the *Pietà*. Now that we have settled on the abiding image we are going to explore—those bags of groceries my boyfriend left on our kitchen table—our next task is not to write a poem, but to create a big old messy hunk of stone. Our hunk of stone, however, unlike the one Michelangelo always started with, will not be made of marble, but of words.

When I sit down to create my hunk of stone, I allow myself to write into the mystery of my abiding image. I am also allowing myself to play, to romp, and to run; to explore the world of sound and taste and sight and touch and smell—for it is these senses that poems are made of, not ideas and abstractions and profound meanings. The idea or theme or meaning will eventually make itself known, but right now that is not my business. My business is to become a child again, to open myself to all the mysterious layers wrapped around that abiding image longing to be explored.

> If my name were a color it would be brown like the bags of groceries my boyfriend left on Mama's kitchen table every Friday night after my family broke up.

I have had my morning coffee and have just sat down to create a messy hunk of stone. Even after almost thirty years of writing poems, I still have to remind myself that this stage of the writing experience is about *process* not *product*. Now is not the time for dictionaries and thesauruses, for worrying about sentence structure or punctuation. Now is the time to hang around for a while in our intuitive minds, our right brains. The ancient Greeks would have called it evoking the energies or powers of Dionysus, the god of wine and revelry, of chaos and mystery, of darkness and instinct. We'll call on the energies of the left-brain powers of Apollo later when the time is right, when we are ready to assess and discern the insights and surprises Dionysus has revealed to us.

The room is quiet and I'm ready to explore. I begin by writing everything I can remember about those bags and the groceries inside—the way they looked and smelled. How the paper and the boxes and the cans felt in our hands. All the sounds my memory might conjure in relation to those bags of groceries that were always there for us when we walked sleepy-eyed and groggy into the kitchen on Saturday mornings. And then, best of all, the taste of what was inside.

I remember the coarse brown paper those Piggly Wiggly bags were made of, the little pigs' heads circled in red. The dinette table, white enamel with red trim around the ledge, the red and white plastic-covered chairs with metal legs. The images keep coming, flooding me with distant sounds of the passing train, the boxcars that carried the unbleached muslin to the bleachery to be finished into lovely sheets and pillow cases and bolts of colorful fabric. Memories of the mill whistle signaling the end of a long, hard shift in the weave room or spinning room. My mother coming in late and tired from her new job as nursing assistant at the old-folks' home, yelling at me and my sister because we had not picked up the wet towels our brothers had left on the bathroom floor. And, ah, those little clandestine trips with my boyfriend down to the railroad tracks after my exhausted mother had finally gone to bed.

Image after image after image continues to pour forth, the words streaming uninhibited and uncensored across the pages from the left margin all the way to the right. This is, indeed, a mess. The words are clunky and awkward, the phrases practically indiscernible. This looks nothing like a poem, just string after string of words and phrases making their way from one side of the page to the other like a drunken and disorderly conga line. And, God, the clichés, the trite language, the jargon! But I know if I start censoring those things, I will also automatically start censoring the good stuff. So I let it all fall onto the page as memory begets memory and I continue to be lost in my writer's trance until . . . until a memory that has been languishing for years in the depths of my unconscious tumbles onto the page—a detail about those groceries I had totally forgotten; the detail that reveals to me the metaphorical gift of this abiding image; the detail that makes me realize that the real subject—the tenor—of this poem is not those bags of groceries at all, but the family itself, the groceries simply the vehicle that helped get me to the real subject of the poem; the detail that makes me realize why, of all the images I experienced during that difficult time, this was the one that attached itself to me and would not let go—like those beggar lice hitching their free ride on my socks and cuffs after rambles through those long-ago childhood meadows. This is the detail that helps me see, finally, the poem that is there inside my messy hunk of stone—the poem waiting to be chiseled and shaped and polished—like the *David* or the *Pietà*.

The detail about those groceries I had totally forgotten? They were not just bags of groceries brought home by my boyfriend to help my broken family survive. They were damaged goods: torn boxes of cereals and detergents; cans whose labels had been sliced away by the blade of a careless box-cutter; bent tins of vegetables and fruits; split bags of dried beans and rice. Damaged goods. Just like my family.

How surprised we always were when the night's three-can ration yielded three cans of pickled beets or three cans of pineapple or a trio of beans—lima, black-eyed peas, and pintos.

Not the most well-balanced meals, but ones we were always glad to get. Yes, we were, indeed, a damaged family, like the groceries we would continue to eat those first few difficult months. Damaged goods that would help ensure our survival. A family, who, because of this gift, would not only *endure*, as William Faulkner once said, but *prevail*.

My hunk-of-stone stage is completed. I am now ready to begin cutting and shaping and polishing this mess into a poem.

Come with me and watch my poem emerge. . . .

FOUR

Cutting and Shaping and Polishing

Once I gave myself permission to make a mess, the image of those bags of groceries sitting on our kitchen table each Saturday morning after my Friday-night date evolved into seven pages of scribble. I had allowed myself to write into the mystery of that image. And once I realized that the *story* of the poem seemed to be about not only the damaged family but about that family's enduring and prevailing, I knew which words and phrases I could chip away and which ones I could tweak and polish for an even more resonant recreation of an image that had haunted me for years.

First, I cut anything that hinted of cliché or sentimentality. All the *tears* had to go. All the *broken hearts*. I can't remember who said, "If you really want to move your reader, be cold," but I try hard to adhere to that dictum. Then I went through the mess and marked out anything that did not echo or hint at the theme of destruction followed by transcendence. I loved the image of my brothers throwing their wet towels on the bathroom floor during those early days of our harsh father's absence, but since nobody was terrified enough to even pick them up and toss them into the laundry basket, that image had to go. My sister's jealousy of my relationship with my grocery-stealing boyfriend also had to go.

Next I took a microscopic look at individual word choice. The *blanket* the speaker took into the boxcar became a *quilt*. Why? Blankets are just blankets. Quilts are, truly, transcendent objects, having been created out of scraps and pieced together into something new and beautiful and comforting. The original phrase *helped me down from the boxcar* became *lift[ed] me down again onto the gravel and took me home*. And *when the whistle blew* became *when the whistle signaled third shift free*. The word *taped* became *bandaged*.

So, I had whittled and smoothed and polished the mess, and was, at least for the time being, satisfied enough to turn my attention to *line*. How could I best put this poem on the page so that line length, line and stanza breaks, etc., might enhance further the *feeling, story*, and *language* of the poem.

I must admit that when I was writing this poem, I was still pretty ignorant of the strategies more practiced and studied poets wield when thinking about this aspect of the poem (Think Nick Flynn's "Bag of Mice" discussed at length in Chapter One). But going on instinct, I decided to use lots of run-on lines, starkly enjambed, and one unbroken stanza; for time, at that point in our lives, seemed a bombardment—a breathless blur of sounds and tastes and textures and smells and sights. We had leapt out of the cauldron of fear and dread into another cauldron of fear and dread. But one, too, of freedom and hope and grace.

Robert Frost once said, "A poem is never finished. We just reach a point at which we choose to abandon it." I give you, now, that poem:

Groceries

I had a boyfriend once, after my mother
and brothers and sisters and I
fled my father's house, who worked
at the Piggly Wiggly where he stocked
shelves on Fridays until midnight
then drove to my house to sneak me out,
take me down to the tracks by the cotton mill
where he lifted me and the quilt I'd brought
into an empty boxcar. All night

the wild thunder of looms. The roar of trains
passing on adjacent tracks hauling
their difficult cargo, cotton bales
or rolls of muslin on their way
to the bleachery to be whitened, patterned
into stripes and checks, into still-life gardens
of wisteria and rose. And when the whistle
signaled third shift free, he would lift me
down again onto the gravel and take me home.
If my mother ever knew she didn't say, so glad
in her new freedom, so grateful for the bags
of damaged goods stolen from the stockroom
and left on our kitchen table. Slashed
bags of rice and beans he had bandaged
with masking tape, the labelless cans,
the cereals and detergents in varying
stages of destruction. Plenty
to get us through the week, and even some plums
and cherries, tender and delicious,
still whole inside the mutilated cans
and floating in their own sweet juice.

Though "Groceries" is one of my earlier poems, I never tire of reading it to anyone gracious enough to listen. I also never tire of comments offered from audience members about aspects of the poem that had some special resonance for them. My favorite such observation came from someone who found the phrase *damaged goods* especially intriguing—on yet another metaphorical level. He reminded me that this phrase was once (and probably still is in some mindsets) applied derogatorily to a female who has had sexual relations without the benefit of matrimony. He drew my attention to the sexual connotations of the words *cherries, tender and delicious . . . floating in their own sweet juice.*

Sex for food. Sex as a means of survival for a family in crisis.

I was stunned. That connection had not occurred to me as I was exploring the abiding image of those groceries. But more than stunned, I was excited! Why? Because yet again does a single poem give evidence to the saying that the poem is smarter than we are. And yet again does this poetic process give evidence to the verity of something I once heard my friend and colleague Joyce Rockwood Hudson say: "The kingdom of heaven is within, and it is a dialogue between the conscious and the unconscious." When we begin with a single abiding image and allow ourselves to write into the mystery of that image, we are, indeed, setting up a dialogue between the conscious and the unconscious. A dialogue that can reveal insights the poet never even knew she had, that are sometimes so subtle it takes an insightful reader or listener to point them out to her.

FIVE

The Role of Tension in Poetry

After my first husband divorced me, I sat down with an abiding image centered around an old truck he adored. The truck was so scary and erratic and decrepit I dubbed it *Satanic Ritual.* One day we were barreling down a narrow country road when he grabbed the gear stick to down-shift. Already fearing for my life, I saw that the gear stick had pulled loose and he was holding it in midair as we screeched and rattled around a hairpin curve. *This is it,* I thought, *I'm dead,* then leaned back and closed my eyes, preparing to meet my maker. When I realized I was still in this world, I opened them again and looked at him. The gear stick was still in his hand, and his face glowed with the most euphoric expression I had ever witnessed. I knew from experience that frolicking through his mind were visions of an entire weekend doing whatever it might take to restore his beloved Satanic Ritual to its previous decrepitude.

Several years had passed when I sat down with this abiding image, my goal being to poke fun at (aka, exact vengeance on) my ex. I laughed my way through my first few pages of mess until an especially surprising line drifted up from my unconscious:

I loved him for his love of broken things . . .

It was then my laughter ceased. I burst into tears. I remembered, suddenly, how when we met—both of us still in our teens—I, myself, was a *broken thing,* and he, that boy who had stocked shelves at the Piggly Wiggly on Friday nights; that boy who had helped save my shattered family's life with those brown paper bags filled with their weekly assortment of damaged goods.

Allowing myself to begin with a single abiding image—the euphoric look on my young husband's face as he navigated Satanic Ritual around those tortuous curves while brandishing the derelict gear stick like a trophy above our heads—helped me set free all those warring emotions I had for so long suppressed.

So, the poem that was meant to be a satirical exploration of a single absurd moment in a marriage, became an exploration of a vast complex of emotions: frustration, terror, and resentment, all tangled up with the conflicting emotions of tenderness, gratitude, regret, and love. In other words, the poem became an exercise in tension, an element crucial to any of the sophisticated arts.

Creative tension has always been a major concern for serious artists. Artists during Greece's fifth century BCE, for example, strove to bring together in their sculptures, architecture, and theatrical performances a perfect juxtaposition of opposites—the chaotic, passionate, intuitive energies of Dionysus (god of revelry and wine) with the orderly, rational, intellectual energies of Apollo (god of prophecy, sunlight, and music). A good example of this Greek wielding of tension can be seen in the friezes of the Parthenon. These friezes are made up of alternating bas-relief depictions of chaotic battle and festival scenes separated at equal intervals by blocks of three orderly vertical grooves known as triglyphs. Such achievement—especially in this level of perfection with artistic tension—is why this period is still referred to as Greece's Golden Age.Except for writers of Hallmark verse, a skillful use of tension is still a major concern of poets. Please know, however, that my intention is not to denigrate what I refer to as Hallmark verse. I buy Hallmark cards all the time. But when I am looking for just the right Hallmark card to send to a loved one, the last thing I want to create is more tension for that person. Indeed, rather than evoking for the recipient of my card a bombardment of disparate emotions, what I really want to do is evoke for him or her a single emotion: sympathy, or pride, or joy, or gratitude. I wish, as a matter of fact, I could write Hallmark verse. I would be making a hell of a lot more money than I'm making.

So, for those poets who do aspire to a certain level of tension in our poems, who want to engage our readers in the emotional and intellectual life of the poem, I offer two simple definitions of this thing known as artistic tension: the pulling against each other of opposites, and the upsetting of the reader's expectations. In writing a poem, we can create or enhance the tension in all four aspects of the poem—feeling, story, language, and line.

One way of making sure tension is present in the *feeling* and *story* of the poem is to begin with—yes—an abiding image. As I mentioned in Chapter Two, there has to be something about that image—*the smell of a quinine covered thumb, the warmth of a pine-knot fire, the sizzle of country ham frying on grandmother's black wood stove*—that has caused it to *abide* with us. Something about our immediate emotional response to that particular sight, sound, smell, taste, or texture has made it *stick*. I have come to realize that entangled within those seemingly surface moments is a deeper well of feelings, often disparate emotions pulling against each other. Allowing our selves to write into the mystery of that abiding image by first creating a mess will bring into dialogue two other forces often at odds with each other: the conscious and the unconscious.

Now, back to the abiding image that set into motion this discussion of artistic tension: the euphoric look on my husband's face when Satanic Ritual's gear stick pulled loose in his hand. As I wrote into the mystery of that image, creating my messy *hunk of stone* without judging or questioning or editing myself, all kinds of strange images drifted up from my unconscious: the biblical Jonah in the belly of his whale; Van Gogh's vibrant, pulsating paintings; the pre-Socratic philosopher Heraclitus and his famous assessment of the human experience—*You can't step into the same river twice.* And before I knew what was happening, even a beleaguered Jesus had found his way into the muddle.

When I finally decided my making-a-mess stage had exhausted itself, I went into discernment mode, to assess and clean up all the ostensible odds and ends that had congregated on my pages. Of the dozens of other seemingly nonsensical images that drifted up out of my unconscious, only the aforementioned Jonah, Van Gogh, Heraclitus, and Jesus made the final cut. Why? Because letting the unconscious exhaust itself by making a mess revealed to me the bigger, archetypal themes that roiled inside and beyond that original surface image. I was writing a poem about the cyclical nature of things—life, death, and rebirth; a poem about that old human desire for stasis and the contradictory truth Heraclitus observed: that life in this world is in a constant state of flux; that the human condition, even in the realm of till-death-do-us-part romantic love, is one of inevitable change.

As I began to craft my mess into a poem—keeping in mind this bigger *story* that had revealed itself to me—I took a microscopic look at the *language* I was using. Allowing myself now to do further brainstorming with the help of the unabridged dictionary and thesaurus, I worked hard to enhance the tension in the language by using unpredictable or contradictory word choices, words that resonate on several different levels instead of only one. *When I heard the sound of my husband's truck* became *When I heard the sudden thunder of my husband's truck*. Unlike the relatively flat word *sound*, the word *thunder* suggests several levels of meaning. We associate thunder with (at least) two disparate forces—both lightning, that can bring about destruction, and rain, that can bring about new life.

I also paid close attention to the sounds of the words I was using. I wanted to end my poem on a note of tenderness, so I tweaked my final sentence and incorporated three words containing the low-tension vowel sounds *uh* and *oo*—*lovers, love, moon*. I concluded the poem with the word *falling*, another low-tension vowel sound, *ah*, with a final unaccented syllable that creates a further softening effect. Quite a shift from the tough, muscular sounds dominating the opening lines of the poem: *When I heard the sudden / thunder of my husband's truck / explode into the drive.* (Chapter Six will take a more thorough look at the effects of vowel tensions and syllabics.)

Such discerning attention to language can often result in the creation of metaphor. Whenever we incorporate metaphor in our poems, we automatically enhance the tension by asking the reader to hold in his or her mind—and at the same time— a juxtaposition of opposites. As I pushed the language toward more resonant word choices, [*the*] *open hood* of my husband's truck became *its open wound of primer*. The phrase *open wound* suggests, simultaneously, both the truck's injury and the possible healing of that injury through my husband's painstaking and passionate tinkering. And often, the more disparate the two things being compared, the more dramatically *upset* the reader's expectations. Who could be more different from my truck driving ex-husband than the aforementioned cast of characters who made their way into the poem—Jonah, Van Gogh, Heraclitus, and Jesus? Yet each, in his own way, informs the feeling and story of the poem on a metaphorical level, thus enhancing even further the poem's tension.

Shifting sentence structures is another way of using language to create tension. I decided to begin my poem with an eleven-line complex sentence made up of a long subordinate clause full of prepositional phrases followed by the simple declarative clause *I knew how the evening would go.* I followed this long complex sentence with another long—seven line—fragment made up of another bombardment of phrases. Just when my reader expects a continuation of this syntactical strategy, I upset that expectation with a short, one-line simple declarative sentence: *I loved him for his love of broken things.*

Not only can tension be enhanced in the feeling, story, and language of the poem, but also in the *line* of the poem—the way the poem is arranged on the page. We can, for instance, use stanza and line enjambment—forcing the reader into the next line or stanza instead of allowing him or her to pause at those places. Our old literary brains tell us to expect a rest or stop at the end of the line and the end of the stanza. Even the modern poet Robert Frost sometimes adhered to this traditional strategy. Think "Stopping by Woods on a Snowy Evening":

> Whose woods these are I think I know.
> His house is in the village, though;
> He will not see me stopping here
> To watch his woods fill up with snow.

We stop exactly where we expected to stop, don't we? (Pun delightfully unintended.) To create tension in my own poem—and to enhance the feeling of that unstoppable flow of things, Heraclitus's *state of constant flux* idea—I decided, by using enjambment, to give my reader something other than the traditionally expected line breaks. Here is my poem:

You Can't Drive the Same Truck Twice
for my ex-husband

> When I heard the sudden
> thunder of my husband's truck
> explode into the drive
> and saw him, after ramming
> the defective gear stick
> into neutral, emerge crazy-eyed
> and fevered, fling up
> the battered hood, go down
> and disappear beneath its open wound
> of primer, I knew how the evening
> would go. How deep into moonlight
> he would hang like Jonah, half in,
> half out, his full weight given
> to the wrench, gripped to the stripped
> bolts and nuts, capping and uncapping
> the ancient battery, his body
> lost to that odd carcass of scavenged parts.
> I loved him for his love of broken things.
> The handleless hoes and axes, the sprung

rumble seat bought years ago
at auction, the legless chairs
retrieved from garbage heaps,
that truck each day he reinvented.
Like the rivers of Heraclitus. Like Van Gogh's
olive trees and irises that quiver,
still. Bristle. As if caught forever
in the antique instant of their opening.
It's why we love Jesus, some philosopher
once said, instead of God. Why lovers
love the moon that's always falling.

————

A poem that continues to haunt me is James Wright's "Saint Judas." Every aspect of Wright's poem—feeling, story, language, and line—radiates tension. Notice your body's visceral reaction as you read it.

Saint Judas

When I went out to kill myself, I caught
A pack of hoodlums beating up a man.
Running to spare his suffering, I forgot
My name, my number, how my day began,

How soldiers milled around the garden stone
And sang amusing songs; how all that day
Their javelins measured crowds; how I alone
Bargained the proper coins, and slipped away.

Banished from heaven, I found this victim beaten,
Stripped, kneed, and left to cry. Dropping my rope
Aside, I ran, ignored the uniforms:
Then I remembered bread my flesh had eaten,
The kiss that ate my flesh. Flayed without hope,
I held the man for nothing in my arms.

The title of the poem itself is a juxtaposition of opposites, an upsetting of the reader's expectations. The biblical Judas has long been a symbol of betrayal, monetary greed, and spiritual wretchedness. When we see the name *Judas* preceded by the word *Saint,* we experience a kind of visceral discombobulation on both the conscious and the unconscious level.

So, we enter the *story* of the poem with *feelings* of perplexity and puzzlement. And those feelings intensify as we experience vicariously Wright's imagined "sequel" to the *story*, a heartbreaking scene that explores what might have happened between Judas's betrayal of Jesus and his actual suicide by hanging.

Wright wields *language* in a way that dramatically enhances the poem's tension. In line two we are asked to balance the tension between a centuries-old biblical scene with the contemporary word *hoodlums.* And three lines later, we are presented with a line that, for me at least, is especially mystifying. No biblical scholar myself, something had always haunted me each time I read the line *How soldiers milled around the garden stone*. There was something both familiar and strange about this line. I shared my reaction to this line with my poetry class one day and was enlightened by one student's brilliant recall of this bible verse:

> *It would be better for him to have a millstone hung around his neck and to be thrown into the sea than to cause one of these little ones to stumble.* Luke 17:2

So Wright's line containing the separate words *milled* and *stone* plays a kind of surreal trick on us as we read. The words haunt us in a way we don't quite understand, intensifying the emotions already warring inside us.

And then there is Wright's intriguing use of chiasmus in the lines *I remembered bread my flesh had eaten, / The kiss that ate my flesh*. Chiasmus is the literary technique of repeating a phrase but reversing, in the second phrase, the order of the words: *my flesh had eaten / that ate my flesh*. Our minds, once again, are being pulled in two different directions at the same time.

The final line of Wright's poem: *I held the man for nothing in my arms* is both heartbreaking and redemptive—yet another example of Wright's use of language to evoke powerfully disparate emotions. The phrase *for nothing* can be taken in two different ways. Judas's kiss on Jesus's cheek was done for monetary gain—a cache of silver coins. The final act of holding in his arms a dying man will receive, however, no remuneration. Neither will the act gain Judas any points with his God, who has already banished him from heaven. Judas has, indeed, in more ways than one, *held the man for nothing in [his] arms.*

In the aspects of *feeling, story,* and *language,* Wright not only upsets the reader's expectations, but asks the reader to hold in balance a bombardment of opposites. But my greatest surprise and delight—after having read this poem dozens of times—was in discovering what Wright has done with *line,* or, in this case, the structure of the poem. The poem is, indeed, a sonnet. An even closer look revealed Wright's use of a strategically fluctuating iambic pentameter line and a deft use of line enjambment to soften the rhyme scheme.

I looked closely at the end words of stanzas one and two: **caught, man, forgot, began, stone, day, alone, away.** *Ah,* I thought, *a-b-a-b . . . c-d-c-d, an English sonnet.* But that expectation was turned on its head when I looked at the end words of stanza three: **beaten, rope, uniforms, eaten, hope, arms.** The English sonnet rhyme scheme I had expected of these final lines, e-f-e-f-g-g, was not there. Instead, Wright had brought his poem to a close with a variation on the Italian rhyme scheme, e-f-g-e-f-g.

"So are you saying," a student once asked, "that Wright betrayed us just as Judas betrayed Jesus?"

Perhaps artistic tension is, after all, just that—a kind of betrayal. But a good betrayal in that its presence in a work of art requires us as readers—or listeners or viewers—to take full part in the emotional and intellectual urges that impelled the artist to this particular act of creation. A betrayal that asks us to see in a different way everything we thought we knew or understood about being human. That recalls, once again, author Thomas Moore's assertion that *the beast at the center of the labyrinth is*, indeed, *also an angel.*

Even if that angel had once been dubbed *Satanic Ritual* by its owner's remorsefully sardonic but always grateful ex.

SIX

The Use of Sound and Syllabics to Create and Illuminate Meaning

On the first day of my senior year in high school, I found myself under the tutelage of what seemed a ninety-year-old English teacher who hunched at the front of the class and mumbled to the few students close enough to hear what she was saying. Unfortunately (or fortunately as it turns out), being a Smith, I had once again been alphabetized to the back of the room with the even more unfortunate *T, U, V, W, X, Y,* and *Zs.* One day (I think it was day two) I finally just gave up and started randomly flipping through my literature book, perusing the vast storehouse of poems that had accumulated over the past one thousand five hundred and eighteen years, upon one of which my eyes came to rest—

> I caught this morning morning's minion, king-
> dom of daylight's dauphin, dapple-dawn-drawn
> Falcon, in his riding
> Of the rolling level underneath him steady air, . . .

I was hooked.

Every day as the teacher mumbled on about some goblin and his green knight, I would spend the hour pouring over these words and the others that followed. I walked the halls amidst the opening and clanging shut of lockers, quietly reciting the entire text of this enigmatic poem called "The Windhover," written by that even more enigmatic poet called Gerard Manley Hopkins: *I caught this morning morning's minion, king- / dom*

*of daylight's dauphin, dapple-dawn-drawn Falcon in his riding
/ Of the rolling level underneath him steady air . . .*

Did I have any idea what those words meant? Noooo . . .
Did I get asked out on any dates during that year? Noooo . . .

All I did know was that there was something going on inside those words that was working on my body, my heart, and my soul. I had fallen in love not with the meaning of those words, but with the sound and the rhythm of those words. My obsession with Hopkins' work grew, though it would be many years before I allowed myself to ask: *Could these beautiful words actually mean anything?* It would be even more years before an in-depth study of sound and rhythm would help me understand the powerful impact of these elements, not only on the emotional level of the reader or listener, but on the physiological level.

So strongly do I believe we should first honor the sounds a poem elicits, I begin every poetry class or workshop by reading to my students several of my favorite poems; poems whose words I love to feel and hear issuing across my tongue and through my lips—Hayden's "Those Winter Sundays," Brooks' "We Real Cool," Bishop's "The Fish," Neruda's "Ode to My Socks," Kate Barnes' "Imagining It." But before I begin reading, I share with them Robert Bly's belief that when we read a poem on the page, we take it into our heads, and when we hear it, we take it into our bodies. So, I have deliberately not given them copies of the poems I am about to read. "Do not think about the meaning of the words," I say. "That will come later. Let the words wash over you. Notice your visceral reaction to the words—how the words make you *feel* on the body level."

Oh, how I wish I'd had a teacher who introduced a poem in this manner rather than instructing me to read the poem on page 3,999 of the literature book and write a paragraph explaining what it means. Wouldn't it be lovely to enter a poem in a less intimidating way? To allow ourselves to be swept away by the sounds the words make until there is an actual reason to give a hoot whether those words mean anything or not?

I caught this morning morning's minion, king- . . .

When a poem does something to every cell of my being, or, as Emily Dickinson said to Thomas Wentworth Higginson, "makes me feel so cold no fires could ever warm me," I want to know how the poet has done that to me. And it always—yes, I said *always*—comes down to sound rather than meaning. At this point, however, I offer a bit of cautionary advice: write a long time on instinct before thinking too scientifically about sound. Our good instincts for the sounds of words will serve us quite well when it comes to choosing the right ones. It's why we were drawn to poetry in the first place. And even when you do gain some knowledge as to the machinations of sound, try to keep that knowledge at bay until the later crafting. Sound should be viewed only in revision, and changes made to support sound come in those later stages of writing. In revision, a scientific knowledge of sound might keep you from floundering around for weeks trying to decide between the words *closure* or *closing* as I did decades ago when struggling with one of my poems.

When I feel my students are ready not only to survive but to be excited about journeying into the science of sound, I invite them back to two of the poems I read on the first day of workshop, two classics that illustrate wonderfully how poets can make use of vowel sounds, consonant sounds, units of power, and syllabics to help create and illuminate meaning: Gwendolyn Brooks' "We Real Cool" and Robert Hayden's "Those Winter Sundays." Let us begin with Gwendolyn Brooks' "We Real Cool." Read the poem slowly, out loud (no pen or pencil in hand), noticing its visceral effects on the body.

We Real Cool

The Pool Players.
Seven at the Golden Shovel.

We real cool. We
Left school. We

Lurk late. We
Strike straight. We

Sing sin. We
Thin gin. We

Jazz June. We
Die soon.

Several adjectives come to mind when I think of the powerful feelings this poem arouses in me: *arrogant, haughty,* and *smug.* But tugging against all those passionate and energetic intimations of immortality is the stark shock of reality, even doom—the eventual downfall and early demise to which this kind of reckless attitude can lead. The ancient Greeks called it *hubris,* or excessive pride, a key ingredient in the psychological makeup of their tragic heroes and heroines. Gwendolyn Brooks' brilliant use of vowel sounds helps recreate in the reader a visceral experience of the classic tragic fall.

In casual conversation we tend to stay somewhere in the midrange of vowel sounds—*tug, girl, cat, fret, hit*—since these sounds require less work by the physical body (the lips, the tongue, the throat) to articulate. But one thing that sets poetry apart from prose is that poetry more often takes advantage of the extremes of sound that vowel tensions can offer the writer. The highest vowel frequency sounds in the English language are the long *e—see,* the long *a—say,* and the long *i—sigh.* These sounds can create feelings of excitement, vitality, energy, intensity, even violence—the ostensible attitude toward life of the seven pool players at the Golden Shovel to whom Brooks attributes her poem's bombastic proclamation.

With the first two words of not only the title but of the first line of the poem, *We real*, Brooks puts us right up there at the top of the frequency scale. Appropriate, since the pool players are at the peak of life. But with the third word, *cool*, she plummets us—along with them—to the bottom by making use of one of the lowest frequency vowel sounds *oo*. The low-frequency vowel sounds in descending order—*far, cow, toy, bought, look, bone*—can create feelings of awe, calm, and comfort. Read these short words aloud and notice how the tongue relaxes and the throat opens as the mouth releases the tension required by the previously mentioned high-frequency vowel sounds. Feel how the tension evoked by these low-frequency vowel sounds diminishes at the gut level as you move down the scale of frequencies.

But, as is the case with Brooks' poem, these low-frequency vowel sounds (as well as the high frequency sounds) can have a kind of bi-polar effect by simultaneously creating feelings of sadness, dread, weight, and gloom. Brooks' use of this strategy is relentless. With every three-word sentence, she keeps putting us back on top of the world with the repetition of the word *We*, then sends us tumbling again to the bottom where we land, finally, on the word *soon.* Consonant sounds can also have a powerful effect on a reader's visceral response. The consonant sounds long considered by many poets as the most pleasing in the English language are the *r* and the *l*. Though all of the consonant sounds require more physical effort to make than any of the vowel sounds, the *r* and the *l* are the least physically taxing consonant sounds to make (*r*, as a matter of fact, is considered by many linguists, along with *w*, a vowel). These are called *liquids*, since, unlike the other consonants, they do not require a cutting off of air flow to make. Notice that although Brooks does make use of these liquids—there are six *l*s and four *r*s—they occur in the first half of the poem.

> We real cool. We
> Left school. We
>
> Lurk late. We
> Strike straight. We

The more dire the prospects become for these seven cocky pool players, the less *lovely* the consonant sounds. Lines two and three contain two *plosives* each, *t* and *k* in line two, and *k* and *t* in line three. The plosives—that also include *p, b, d,* and *g*—actually stop the airflow momentarily, then the air is released again with a little ex-*plosion* of sorts. So in the midst of all those easy liquid *r*s and *l*s, the poet has already begun to kick us awake with a bombardment of *k*s and *t*s.

In the second half of the poem, there is a prevalence of not only the aforementioned plosives, but also the consonant sounds known as *fricatives* (*h, f, c, th, s, z, sc, sn*). These sounds require only a partial cutting off of the breath in order to pronounce them. Notice the repetition of the *s* sound, a fricative that requires the tongue and teeth to force air through a tight space, resulting in a hissing sound.

> Strike straight. We
> Sing sin. We
> Thin gin. We
>
> Jazz June. We
> Die soon.

Besides Brooks' effective use of sound in this poem, her artistry with syllabics, or units of power, is just as masterful in helping to illuminate meaning. The entire poem is made up of monosyllabic words, a structural unit that can imply, among other things, firmness, roughness, danger, hardness, and obstinacy—all ostensible qualities of these pool players who will, before their natural time, find themselves at the most obstinate place of all: *death*, yet another monosyllabic word.

"The sound must seem an echo to the sense," Alexander Pope says in his "Essay on Criticism." What better testament to that poetic truth than Brooks' huge little poem "We Real Cool."

One would be hard put to find a poem that emanates a more disparate tone from Brooks' poem than Robert Hayden's sonnet "Those Winter Sundays," another masterful wielding of sound and syllabics to create and illuminate meaning. Read the poem slowly and out loud, noticing its effect on the visceral level.

Those Winter Sundays

Sundays too my father got up early
and put his clothes on in the blueblack cold,
then with cracked hands that ached
from labor in the weekday weather made
banked fires blaze. No one ever thanked him.

I'd wake and hear the cold splintering, breaking.
When the rooms were warm, he'd call,
and slowly I would rise and dress,
fearing the chronic angers of that house,

Speaking indifferently to him,
who had driven out the cold
and polished my good shoes as well.
What did I know, what did I know
of love's austere and lonely offices?

I have been known to joke that the only reason I teach is so I can read and discuss this poem with an intelligent, sensitive group of people who honor the power of words. Although I have read this poem hundreds and hundreds of times, it never fails to send goosebumps from the bottom of my feet to the top of my skull. As opposed to the sense of arrogance, haughtiness, smugness, and impending doom I feel each time I read Brooks' poem "We Real Cool," Hayden's poem engenders a different tangle of emotions— unflinching love, sacrifice, tenderness, and gratitude all wound up with regret and remorse and sorrow and shame. Let's see how Hayden, just as brilliantly as Brooks, wields sound and syllabics to create and illuminate meaning.

The first line of Hayden's poem relies heavily on low-frequency vowels to describe a devoted, caring, comforting father: *Sundays, too, my father got up early* . . . . The line consists of ten vowel sounds, and seven of those are low- to low-middle-frequency sounds. So, we begin our poem with an overriding sense of quiet and calm and tenderness. All the lines of the poem that recreate tender, soothing, loving actions are laden with these lower to mid-frequency vowels:

> When the rooms were warm, he'd call,
> and slowly I would rise and dress . . .
>
> who had driven out the cold
> and polished my good shoes as well

But there is also tension within this household, and it's interesting to note that the lines heaviest with intensity and physical pain are just as laden with high-middle- to high-frequency vowel sounds. Note, especially the prevalence of the long *a*, the second highest frequency vowel sound:

> then with cracked hands that ached
> from labor in the weekday weather made
> banked fires blaze.

Hayden is just as deft a wielder of syllabics to illuminate meaning as he is with sound. Unlike the constant bombardment of monosyllabic words we spoke of earlier in Brooks' "We Real Cool," "Those Winter Sundays" relies heavily on the effect of multisyllabic words. Multisyllabic words have a tendency to soften the emotional impact, creating feelings such as kindness, sympathy, gentleness, and nostalgia. Two of the words in the three-word title are multisyllabic words—*Winter/Sundays*. And half of the six words in the first line are multisyllabics—*Sundays/father/early*. In stanzas two and three, there is even the appearance of several three-syllable (or more) words—*splintering, indifferently,* and *offices.*

The only line in the poem that gives itself completely over to monosyllabic words is the heartbreakingly honest penultimate line, an almost painful cry of *mea culpa*:

> What did I know, what did I know . . .

This line, though, relinquishes itself immediately to the softer, more compassionate, multisyllabic words of the final line:

> . . . of love's austere and lonely offices?

Hayden's poem, unlike Brooks' monosyllabic poem, asks for yet another level of discernment—the effects of rising syllables versus the effects of falling syllables. Multisyllabic words with the accent on the final syllable (*austere* is the only such word in Hayden's poem), create on the visceral level a final burst of energy or force. But Hayden's poem contains nineteen words ending with falling syllables, a diminishment or softening of energy at the end of the word. Two of those words—*lonely offices*—bring the poem to its close with a double-dose of tenderness.

Such artistry with sound and syllabics to create meaning continues to keep Brooks and Hayden—especially in regards to the two poems just discussed—among the most influential of the twentieth century American poets. Perhaps they too had been mesmerized, instructed, and inspired by the sound and syllabics of the inimitable Gerard Manley Hopkins:

> *I caught this morning morning's minion, king-* . . .

SEVEN

A Bit More about Metaphor

Aristotle said that a command of metaphor can be neither learned nor imparted—it is "a sign of genius." I agree with Aristotle that metaphor is a sign of genius. I would also add that each of us comes into this world with that little bit of genius deep inside us.

A few years ago I had the pleasure of having lunch with one of my dearest friends since junior high school. I had not yet met Candy's three-year-old daughter, Suzanne, and was delighted to finally make her acquaintance. In the midst of an energized lunch of good food and boisterous laughter brought on by reminiscences of the good old days, Candy and I suddenly became aware that little Suzanne was desperately attempting to get our attention. We looked down to where she sat in her booster seat to see her flapping back and forth the leftover peel of the banana she had just consumed. "Look, Mommy, look," she was shouting with glee, "I have a yellow fish!"

"Oh, you silly thing," Candy responded. "That's not a yellow fish, it's a banana peel!" But I was quick to disabuse my dear friend of her misguided assessment of the peel still flapping back and forth in her daughter's tiny hand.

"It most certainly is a yellow fish," I said as I picked up another segment of the peel and began flapping it back and forth just as enthusiastically. Before long, Candy, too, had joined in, and there the three of us sat, waving our now browning banana peels above our heads as the other diners looked curiously on at our antics.

How right Aristotle was: a command of metaphor is, indeed, a sign of genius; a genius that accompanies us into a world of well-meaning parents and teachers who, more often than not, proceed to beat it out of us. The unconscious mind, though, as attested to by our nightly dreams, is loathe to let go of that poetic genius—our birthright, old as time itself.

The word metaphor comes from two Greek words: *meta*, which means *above, beyond* or *across* (as in *metaphysical*), and *phor*, which means *to carry* (think *phosphorescence*). So the word metaphor means *to carry across*. The thing that is carried across is a deeper meaning that transcends the literal.

Every metaphor has two parts: the *tenor* and the *vehicle*. The tenor of a metaphor is the subject of actual concern (banana peel). The vehicle is the image that carries the comparison (yellow fish). Our everyday language is rich with metaphor—but more often than not, we have no idea we are using metaphor.

For example, when we see a person aimlessly wandering the streets, we might refer to that person as a *derelict*. Most of us, however, don't know that the word *derelict* really means *an abandoned ship*. So when we refer to someone as a derelict, we are, indeed, using metaphor, for we are comparing that aimless person to an abandoned ship. In this particular metaphor, the tenor is the aimless person (subject of actual concern), and the vehicle (no pun intended!) is the abandoned ship.

A subject poets have been exploring through metaphor, at least as far back as the Greek poet Sappho, is the subject of romantic love. The late eighteenth-century Scottish poet Robert Burns used as the vehicle for his exploration of romantic love that of a red, red rose: "O my Luve's like a red, red rose . . . ." Through the ages, however, the rose metaphor—along with stars, and wine, and symphonies, and warm puppies—has become stale. And since one of the major tasks of the serious poet is to say things in a way they've never been said before, we must continue to push for unexpected, surprising vehicles for our subjects of actual concern.

Notice how former poet laureate of the UK, Carol Ann Duffy (who, like Robert Burns, interestingly enough, is also Scottish), deals with the subject of romantic love:

Valentine

Not a red rose or a satin heart.

I give you an onion.
It is a moon wrapped in brown paper.
It promises light
like the careful undressing of love.

Here.
It will blind you with tears
like a lover.
It will make your reflection
a wobbling photo of grief.

I am trying to be truthful.

Not a cute card or a kissogram.

I give you an onion.
Its fierce kiss will stay on your lips,
possessive and faithful
as we are,
for as long as we are.

Take it.
Its platinum loops shrink to a wedding-ring,
if you like.
Lethal.
Its scent will cling to your fingers,
cling to your knife.

Duffy's use of the onion vehicle allows her to explore the subject of romantic love with unsentimental honesty. By looking at all characteristics of the onion—both the pleasant and the not-so-pleasant—she has created what is known as an extended metaphor, or *conceit*. Her main vehicle for love is the onion, but then she goes on to call up a series of vehicles for the onion itself: a moon, a lover, a photo, a kiss, a wedding ring, a scent that clings. Notice that these many vehicles are reminiscent of the romantic side of love, but a closer look at Duffy's images reveals another side of each vehicle—a darker, more realistic view of romantic love. The moon comes in a not-so-romantic wrapping of *brown paper*; the lover *will blind you with tears*; the photo is *a wobbling photo of grief*; the kiss *fierce*; the wedding ring bears the stigma of a kind of shrinkage; the scent that clings to the lover's fingers is *Lethal*, and is a scent that also clings to the knife with its ostensible portent of danger.

One of my favorite poems that makes use of a delightful catalogue of fresh metaphors is Robert Bly's translation of Pablo Neruda's "Ode to My Socks." Read the poem—out loud if possible—letting the poem's magical use of metaphor wash over and through you.

Ode to My Socks

Mara Mori brought me
a pair of socks
which she knitted herself
with her sheepherder's hands,
two socks as soft as rabbits.
I slipped my feet into them
as if they were two cases
knitted with threads of twilight and goatskin,
Violent socks,
my feet were two fish made of wool,
two long sharks
sea blue, shot through
by one golden thread,
two immense blackbirds,
two cannons,
my feet were honored in this way
by these heavenly socks.
They were so handsome for the first time
my feet seemed to me unacceptable

like two decrepit firemen,
firemen unworthy of that woven fire,
of those glowing socks.

Nevertheless, I resisted the sharp temptation
to save them somewhere as schoolboys
keep fireflies,
as learned men collect
sacred texts,
I resisted the mad impulse to put them
in a golden cage and each day give them
birdseed and pieces of pink melon.
Like explorers in the jungle
who hand over the very rare green deer
to the spit and eat it with remorse,
I stretched out my feet and pulled on
the magnificent socks and then my shoes.

The moral of my ode is this:
beauty is twice beauty
and what is good is doubly good
when it is a matter of two socks
made of wool in winter.

Neruda's catalogue consists of a variety of vehicles for not only these *magnificent socks*, but also his *unworthy* feet. In the end, all of these metaphors help create the meaning or story of the poem—the speaker's deep gratitude and love for the sheepherder who has honored him with this simple and wondrous gift of socks.

I read and discussed this poem once with a lively class of third graders. My niece, Carli Rose, had gotten her teacher's permission to invite me to come and talk to the class about poetry. The students took great delight in calling out the myriads of amazing things to which Neruda compares the socks and his feet: *rabbits, sharks, blackbirds, cannons, firemen, fireflies,* and [birds] *in a golden cage.* They took even more delight when I placed before each of them a large cookie covered in sprinkles—inspiration for their own catalogue of metaphors. Each student began his or her poem in the same way: *Miss Cathy gave me a cookie she had bought with her own good money.* Then they let their imaginations go wild coming up with their own vehicles:

> It was round as_____.
> It was flat as_____.
> It was speckly as_____.
> It crunched in my mouth like_____.
> It disappeared like_____.

Here are some of my favorites these third graders created:

> It was round as Saturn's circles.
> It was flat as a name tag.
> It was speckly as fireworks against the sky.
> It crunched in my mouth like a boot on snow.
> It disappeared like my baby teeth.

And then we ate the cookies, those little geniuses and I!

EIGHT

A Dance of Intensity: The *Minute* Form

In the spring of the turn of the millennium, I was invited to direct a workshop and give a reading at a writers' conference in Oklahoma City. My youngest brother Paul had died a few months earlier after a fourteen-year battle with AIDS. How else to say it other than through the most cliché of clichés—he was the light of our lives. Blessed/cursed with a Richard Corey kind of grace, my brother glittered when he walked, but unlike the enigmatic Corey of Robinson's famous poem, he wanted, more than anything, to live. If such a thing were possible, I would say his death altered my DNA. So I flew from my home in Charlotte, NC, to Oklahoma City, a shadow of the person I once had been, lugging a suitcase full of books and grief.

Since my brother's death I had avoided words, avoided confronting that unspeakable loss. I thought if I extended my visit to Oklahoma City, I might, somehow, in the post-conference quiet of that distant place, allow again into my life the words I had relegated to its periphery.

On the last day of the conference, I attended a reading by a local poet whose name, I regret to say, has escaped me. She began reading a series of poems whose clarity and brevity quickly drew me in. She explained that the poems were written in a form called the *minute*, a poem consisting of sixty syllables with a syllabic line count of 8,4,4,4—8,4,4,4—8,4,4,4. The form also consists of rhyming couplets. I wondered, perhaps, if the rigid mechanics of this form might not provide a safe container for the raw, emotional subject matter now begging to be articulated. I would use the form, I thought, simply to buffer my journey back into the writing life, and eventually back into the world of free verse where, for the last twenty years, I had lived contentedly.

Four years after that conference in Oklahoma City, I remained enamored with the form that still seems an elegant weaving of Elizabethan sonnet and early-Eastern haiku. I wondered if any magazine editors might be open to them and was happily surprised when journals such as *The Atlantic Monthly, The Southern Review,* and *Shenandoah* began to accept them for publication. Soon, my editors at Iris Press suggested I write a whole book of minutes. A little research revealed the creator of this form was Verna Lee Hinegardner, then poet laureate of Arkansas, whose official definition included several elements I was not aware of: a strict iambic meter, capitalization and punctuation like prose, and capturing a slice of life.

My intention at the beginning of every poem was to adhere strictly to rhyme scheme and syllable count. Rarely did I manage to do so, deferring always to sound and sense, rather than to form. What resulted was a collection of adapted minutes—small prayer-like poems, each a reactionary move away from the often cumbersome, complexly cerebral poems that seem, these days, to proliferate in the United States. It is a form that holds me to my own dictum—that our major task in writing a poem is to shine a light on a moment of intensity.

I appropriated for *A Book of Minutes* the structure of *Book of Hours,* the popular devotional book of the Middle Ages. These little prayer books represented a genre that, for the first time in the thirteenth century, put direct access to God into the hands of the laity; an access that until that time had been strictly controlled by those ordained by the Church.

Book of Hours was arranged in accordance with the eight canonical hours of the day: *Matins, Lauds, Terce, Prime, Sext, Nones, Vespers,* and *Compline*—the format I followed in creating *A Book of Minutes.* Each of the eight sections contained a sequence of prayers to be recited at specified hours throughout the day. The first poems I composed for *A Book of Minutes* were poems about my brother's illness and subsequent death. These poems became the penultimate section, *Vespers,* or evening prayers. Here is a sampling from that sequence:

Labor Day

Morning's IV done, all his pills,
he turns to Bill's
gift of Melon—
icy sweet chunks

of honeydew brought home from the
local deli.
I watch each bite
he takes then wipe

his chin. *Unbelievable*, he
says and lifts a
bite to me. Says,
here, just taste this.

The Trunk

I envied my dog that option—
the rattan trunk
chewed this morning
to twig. All night

I had warded off that dream, my
brother alive
once more, asking
if I'd like to

see the trick again. All night, this,
and beyond the
wall, the gnashing
of my dog's teeth.

Torge

Three years after your death, when I
can smile once more,
I recall the
story you loved

to tell, about asking your grade
school teacher to
spell *torge* for you.
Torge? she asked in

sheer bewilderment. *Torge*, you said
again. *Like "The
Prince rode torge the
castle on a*

big white horse."

Watching Bill's New Lover Prepare Our
Evening Meal

Not much, really, has changed. The San
Anselmo sun
streams still into
the room so bright

it almost blinds. And, yes, here still,
the vast array
of kitchen tools
that loved your hands.

See how they glisten now in his.
Dexterous and
able. Almost
as beautiful.

It was always a satisfying experience when I was, indeed, able to adhere to the rule of rhyme and syllable count without compromising sound and sense. "Labor Day" is an example of this success—with, of course, the help of slant-rhymes or half-rhymes: *melon/chunks, he/a,* and *says/this.* This strategy also softened the impact of what is known as *true rhyme.* True rhyme creates a perfect match in the vowel of a stressed syllable and any consonant that follows, as with the rhyme of *pills* and *Bill's* in the same poem.

More often than not, however, I found myself participating in a delicate dance with the form. If I could not, as the form dictated, achieve the appropriate end-rhymes, I might settle, instead, for an internal rhyme. Such is the case with "Watching Bill's New Lover Prepare Our Evening Meal": *into/room* (ll. 3-4), *here/array* (ll. 5-6), *kitchen/hands* (ll. 7-8), *his/ dexterous* (ll. 9-10), and *able/beautiful* (ll. 11-12). I must admit, though, that some of the rhymes were so "slant" I began referring to them simply as "identities." My idea of an identity is exemplified in ll. 3-4 of "The Trunk" with the identification of the "g" in *morning* with the "g" in *twig.* Allowing myself to take such liberties with our traditional notion of rhyme, however, prompted my good students to suggest it might be time for me to purchase a new rhyming dictionary.

Often, rhyme wasn't the only structure I found myself dancing with. The poem "Torge" was written deliberately to fill in the time gap between the poems "The Trunk" and "Watching Bill's New Lover Prepare Our Evening Meal." It was this impetus for the poem, perhaps, that led me away from all pretenses of rhyme and syllable count. The *big white horse* that breaks the boundaries of stanza and syllabic count seemed an appropriate metaphor for my brother's breaking the boundaries between this world and the next.

The whole process, which might seem an exercise in ultimate control, indeed proved otherwise. Ironically, I had to give up much of the control free verse allows—complete power over line-length, stanza, and diction. For four years, my writing practice was obliged to keep a fine balance, at all times during the creative process, between the intuitive and the rational, between reason and emotion, between the head and the heart. This ongoing focus on balance had its effects not only in the writing of poetry, but in the human enterprise of grief. In the writing of this book, I was able to let my beautiful brother go, and to once again experience joy and hope—at times sheer silliness—in a world without him. Such levity in tone can be seen in section four, the sequence that represents the fourth canonical hour *Prime*. Here is one of the poems from that section:

For My Dog, Who Listens to All My Poems

How entranced, each time, she sits there,
her eyes, I swear,
filling with tears
at her master's

inimitable brilliance. It's
clear to me what's
bounding through her
head: *The greatest,*

yet, of all the generations!
My husband says
she's just waiting
for her rations.

If my students had not already suggested it might be time for me to get a new rhyming dictionary, this poem certainly would have warranted that exhortation. The first couplet shows structural promise with the ending perfect rhyme of *there* and *swear.* Then follows, in the next four lines, the off-rhymes of *tears* and *master's* and *It's* and *what's.* Then chaos seems to have tapped me on the shoulder and taken lead of the dance, at least as far as rhyming couplets are concerned. However, do note, in the final stanza, the quirky sound effect created by the end-words of lines 1 and 4: *generations* and *rations*. Dare I claim that these words at least create what is known as a *sight-rhyme?* The editor of the magazine who published this poem said he almost turned the poem down because of that lyrical flaw. But the more times he read the poem, he confessed, the harder he laughed at the comedic tension created by the upsetting of his expectations.

The challenge of this new form—and the gratifications— can be every bit as powerful as traditional forms such as the sonnet, terza rima, villanelle, sestina, and pantoum. Try it. You, too, will enjoy the dance.

NINE

Writing into the Mystery

I used to cringe when I heard my students, after a few days in my creative writing classes, exclaim, "This stuff is great therapy!" I would gather myself into my most academic voice and correct their unfortunate, misguided assessment of my life's work: "This is not therapy. This is art!"

It was not until I read Thomas Moore's book *Care of the Soul*, mentioned in a previous chapter, that I came to realize it was I— not my good students—who was, after all, the misguided one.

It is in this astounding book that Moore reminds us of Socrates' pronouncement that therapy "refers to service to the gods." Perhaps it was the tenuous nature of my past dealings with "the gods" that had made me miss the connection.

I had always envied the stories friends recounted of their religious and spiritual mythologies: calming sticks of Juicy Fruit gum taken quietly from a mother's purse and passed across the Sunday pew; pale aunts speaking, on lavender-scented Wednesday nights, in strange and frightening tongues; fathers carrying sleeping children from Seder to feather bed while the angel passed, as always, over.

I took great pleasure in following up those stories with my own: "My family didn't go to church," I would quip, "we just headed that way." Then I would continue with a dramatized retelling of my father's infrequent and erratic *good spells* when he swore to my mother never to drink again, rousting us from bed the following Sunday, polishing shoes, filling Sunday school envelopes with dimes and quarters, and directing our family of eight up the hill toward Second Baptist, him following proudly in his black suit, improbable hat cocked precariously over his right eye.

But somehow between our house and the church, where others were already ruffling hymnals and settling down into what had long been established as their family pew, my own family would begin its inevitable sloughing off—my brothers lost to some game of marbles sprung up along the way, my sisters to those *awful Snipes boys*, leaning like Jimmy Deans against the white banisters of their porch, me to the novel in my purse or the train rattling down the tracks where I would kneel and press my ear to the rail and hear the devil beat his wife.

This story would always elicit, as I had hoped, a good laugh—the loudest laugh erupting from my own lungs.

After reading Moore's *Care of the Soul,* I realized how much my poetry had given me a spiritual grounding others had found through their own religious and therapeutic paths. For me, writing poetry had been and would continue to be a kind of chronic prayer, a way of looking closely and lovingly enough at the mythologies of my life to realize the truth of Moore's previously mentioned paradox: "the beast residing at the center of the labyrinth is also an angel."

I began praying for a way to share with those outside the academic institution what I was beginning to think of as my *good news*. One day I saw an announcement in the *Charlotte Observer* for a noon-time discussion sponsored by the Haden Institute that would take place the following three Wednesdays. The subject of the discussion was to be none other than Thomas Moore's *Care of the Soul*. Before the three sessions were over, Bob Haden himself had invited me to conduct a six-week poetry workshop using Moore's book as a source of inspiration and guidance for poems to be written by the participants. That six-week workshop turned into two years, and twenty-five years later, I am still spreading, both inside and outside the hallowed walls of my academic institution, my *good news*: One does not have to be a prophet or have several college degrees or an MFA in creative writing to be a poet. I, myself, could have been the poster child for the one least likely to succeed at anything—much less being a *poet.*

I still can't help but smile when someone says to me, "I'm not a poet, but would you please take a look at these poems I wrote and tell me what you think?" I am always honored and delighted to read the poems these *non-poets* have written, but I know already—without even reading them—what I am going to think: Bless you, you glorious human being. You have once again given testimony to Richard Hugo's belief that writing poems "is a way of saying you and the world have a chance."

How true that adage, *We teach what we need to learn.* My prayer to take my good news into the world at large had been answered. I soon became—and remain—a member of the Haden Institute faculty, teaching *The Use of Poetic Expression in Spiritual Direction.* I knew poetry had helped save my life, but I still didn't know *how* it had saved my life. I began searching for clues in the books I was introduced to and in the lectures and seminars of my fellow faculty of priests, therapists, psychologists, scientists, Jungian scholars, anthropologists, Buddhist monks, sociologists, mythologists, and Cirque de Soleil performers. (Okay, just kidding on that last one.) My first big revelation came as I was listening to the previously mentioned Joyce Rockwood Hudson, who lists as her main credential: *Christian laywoman.* Her seminar addressed the human search for wholeness—the journey we embark upon the moment we enter this earthly realm. Putting her own spin on an oft-quoted Jungian concept, "The Kingdom of Heaven is within," she said, "and it is a dialogue between the conscious and the unconscious."

This assessment of Heaven made much more sense to me than the streets paved with gold, the winged angels, and Saint Peter and his pearly gates I had heard about as a child on those rare occasions when I actually made it through the heavy doors of Second Baptist Church. But what made even more sense is that we don't even have to die in order for this *dialogue between the conscious and the unconscious* to take place.

Every time we begin a poem (or embark upon any creative endeavor for that matter), we are opening that dialogue. The process of beginning with a single abiding image and then writing into the mystery of that image by making a mess, by filling the pages, or screens, with my metaphorical big old messy hunks of stone, allows us (*ego*) to step aside and let the unconscious do its job. When we have allowed the unconscious its due time with *feeling* and *story*, then we can let the conscious do its job with *language* and *line*—the crafting part of the process. Now we have set up a dialogue between the conscious and the unconscious, a dialogue that puts us a little more in touch with that *kingdom of heaven within*—that state of wholeness, no matter how short-lived, for which we spend our lives longing.

This process allows us, too, as former dean of Grace Cathedral Alan Jones suggests, "to move from the lust for certainty to the risk of trust"—trusting the abiding image to take us where it needs to take us, instead of where we think it needs to go. No poem I have ever written gives testimony to this mysterious—and sacred—process more powerfully than "The Compass."

The abiding image that triggered this poem was a scene in a small café in Nova Scotia. I was sitting with friends in The Compass Rose—a lovely eatery that featured a compass rose window above our table. I casually commented that I had never understood why compasses were such a big deal—at least for anyone who was traveling in any direction other than north. My companions stared at me dumbfounded for a few moments until my friend Gabe, a forester, proceeded to explain to me exactly how a compass works. I got it! And how delighted I was to realize that a compass could, indeed, be a valuable tool to anyone—no matter the direction in which that person might be traveling.

This moment of enlightenment changed my life, albeit that it happened when I was nearing my fortieth year. I returned home and began my writing morning exploring the abiding image of that scene: the look of disbelief on Gabe's face when

I revealed my misguided assessment of the value of the compass. As I was making my mess of stone, my father, from whom I and my family had long been estranged, found his way onto the page. Thank goodness there was no one in the house at the time to hear me shout: *Get out of here! This is not your poem!* But my father refused to leave, and soon the word *derelict* entered the mess, a word with which I had long been fascinated.

As I said in a previous discussion of metaphor, we use the word *derelict* to describe a bum, a shiftless person. But go back to the origin of the word and we see that it really means *an abandoned ship*. Once that word, accompanied by my estranged father, entered my hunk of stone, I knew I had found my poem. Or it had found me: my father's longing for escape, for freedom, for a better life than the one he had endured in the noise and shadow of the cotton mill—and my own longings that in so many ways paralleled his. I had allowed the unconscious to have its say in the dialogue. I would now let the conscious do the same and begin chiseling away at anything that was not the poem. Ironically, the abiding image that had triggered the poem in the first place went south, which is 180 degrees on the compass—all gone.

I give you my finished—or *abandoned*—poem:

The Compass

When Father finally packed his bag and left
one Sunday after Mother called him a derelict,
I looked up the word in Funk and Wagnall's
and finding that it meant an abandoned ship,
thought how alike we were. Always dreaming
of traveling. Free. Sailing out of that dirty
millyard. Columbus and Vespucci, searching
some secret passage. Lands of spices. Diamonds,
gold and silver. The startled natives
bowing as if we were gods. Next day

in science class, Mr. Hanson gave each of us
a compass to keep, tried to teach us north,
south, east and west. But when he said the compass
always pointed north, my face fell. I glared
at him the rest of the period, wondering
who in his right mind would always want to go
north. An uncle had been there, had warned me
about the place where they mug you in broad
daylight, talk funny, don't understand
real English. I took the compass

home and put it in a drawer beneath the gown
my mother was saving
for when she died. That night I dreamed
of China and Rome, those pink and orange
countries in my geography book, flat paper mountains
my fingers could easily climb, oceans
calm beneath the safe ship of my hand. In the middle

of the night, when I got up to pee, I found my father
slumped, a sunken steamer, across the couch, his suitcase
leaning against the table like a terrible anchor. I
went back to bed, clutching the compass
I had dug from the bottom of the drawer, its smooth glass
sweating in my hand like a flattened globe, and changed
my mind, began planning that slow journey north.

If you could view the early drafts—or messes I fumbled my way
through—you would, perhaps, see how I struggled to replace
my original awkward and mundane word choices with words
that would echo the metaphor of the abandoned ship. What
fun, going to the dictionary and the thesaurus, brainstorming
for words that would echo that sense of traveling, words such
as *sailing, Columbus and Vespucci, some secret passage.* And
later in the poem, the phrases *sunken steamer, terrible anchor,
flattened globe,* and finally *that slow journey north.* These words
and phrases and images all help develop the vehicle of the

metaphor, creating a resonance, a unity, similar to the pleasing repetitions, refrains, etc., in a piece of music.

So, from the abiding image—my derelict father—to the hunk of stone (the work of the unconscious), to the chiseled and crafted poem (the work of the conscious), this process can create in the mind of both writer and reader a sense of order out of chaos. Or, as the previously mentioned Joyce Rockwood Hudson so aptly put it: that feeling of wholeness—that kingdom of heaven within.

Letting my original abiding image of the shocked look on my friend Gabe's face take me where it wanted to go—and not where I had intended for it to go—allowed for a decades-overdue dialogue between the anger and resentment I had harbored on a conscious level toward my father and the empathy, tenderness, and love I had consigned long ago to the unconscious. So, yes, my beloved, not-so-misguided-after-all students, this stuff is, indeed, great therapy.

TEN

Crafting the Dream into Poetry

Poets for centuries have used their dreams as inspiration and subject matter for poems: Samuel Taylor Coleridge, "Kubla Khan"; George Gordon Lord Byron, "The Dream"; John Keats, "Hyperion"; Allen Ginsburg, "Dream Record: June 8, 1955"; and more currently: Mary Oliver, "A Visitor and The Night Traveler"; Nick Flynn, "Bag of Mice"; Mark Doty, "The Embrace"; Sandra Beasely, "I Was the Jukebox." Even the venerable Richard Hugo found inspiration in his own dreams, resulting in his lovely collection *31 Letters and 13 Dreams*. Though I include these works in the large cache of poems I find both inspiring and instructive, I, myself, had always been averse to writing poems from my dreams. Why, I wondered, would a poet find waking life so bereft of sounds, textures, tastes, smells, colors, and shapes that he or she would want to resort to dreams for his or her subject matter?

I had always found the images that appeared in my dreams entertaining, surprising, mesmerizing, sometimes terrifying, often embarrassing: dogs peeing in my hair, slices of watermelon growing along my shin, little fishes swimming around inside my eye. Like many people, I tossed them off as debris from my waking life that had accumulated in the garbage bin of the unconscious. How could anything so crazy as the disjointed, illogical, shape-shifting stuff of my dreams have any purpose at all other than as quirky tidbits to throw into conversations with friends and family? But once I began a serious study of the psychological and spiritual ramifications of dreams, I began to realize how misguided—or unguided—I had always been regarding the phenomenon of dreams and all the powerful ways they might inform and enrich not only our minds and spirits but our creative endeavors as well.

The third-century Jewish Talmadist Rabbi Hisda believed that ignoring a dream is like receiving a letter from God and refusing to open it. And Tertullian, a second-century Christian author from Carthage, asked, "Is it not known to all people that the dream is the most usual way of God's revelation to humankind?" But perhaps Carl Jung (1875–1961), student, then friend, then colleague of Sigmund Freud, remains the most powerful modern proponent of the psychological, spiritual, and intellectual enlightenment that can be experienced when we look closely at our dreams with an informed and discerning eye.

Jung offers us many compelling reasons to see our dreams as a rich storehouse of opportunity for spiritual and psychological growth—for the lifelong process of *individuation*, his word for becoming the human being we were intended to become. He suggests we spend time with a dream that has power and energy for us, that we examine it from every angle and let our imaginations engage with it. What better way, I began to wonder, to let our imaginations engage with a dream than by crafting it into a poem? I set out to do just that and very soon experienced several interesting epiphanies:

- Crafting a dream into a poem renders one of my usual steps in the poetic process null and void. There is no longer any need to make my usual *mess*—the one I fondly refer to as my metaphorical, Michelangelo-inspired, *big old hunk of stone*. The dream itself is my abiding image, and, as dreams are wont to be, it is already a mess. My job is to record, pencil to paper, as faithfully as possible, the mysterious conglomeration of images the dream has gifted me.

- Crafting a dream into a poem reverses my usual strategy of beginning with an abiding image I'm conscious of and then writing into the mystery of all the unconscious has to offer. Beginning with a dream requires me to do the opposite: to lift that unconscious mess of images into consciousness by crafting it into a poem.

· Because my dreams more often than not come to me in such a messy mess, throwing off kilter my waking notions of time and space, reason and logic, the use of traditional forms provides me with a manageable structure through which to bring into dialogue the conscious and the unconscious.

The first dream I crafted into a poem came to me shortly after my father's death. My mother and brothers and sisters and I had been estranged from him for twenty years when he returned sick and dying to our hometown. We gave him a hurried graveside service, grabbed a quick lunch at a Chinese restaurant, then went back to our families and jobs, still harboring a lifetime of resentments and hurts and seemingly unending sorrows. In the dream he appears in the middle of the night at the foot of my bed. I am drowsy and perturbed that he has awakened me, and even more indignant at his request: he wants me to go with him to the gate and talk him into heaven. At this point the dream ends and I am haunted by it for days.

I had, however, in my still-unfolding knowledge of how to work with dreams, learned of a strategy called *carrying the dream forward*. This process of amplification allows the dreamer, during his or her waking hours, to get back into the dream and let the images in the dream continue to manifest. I chose randomly (or so I thought at the time) the form of the English sonnet for my exploration of the dream and of the stunning redemptive images my amplification of the dream engendered.

I set myself the task of fourteen lines, each containing around ten syllables, and the traditional English sonnet rhyme scheme of a-b-a-b, c-d-c-d, e-f-e-f, g-g. I did not attempt to adhere to the traditional iambic pentameter line (five feet of alternating unstressed and stressed syllables), nor did I aspire to the use of perfect rhymes. Perfect rhymes and relentless metrical units are not only old-fashioned, but boring. They also deprive the poem of the element of creative tension discussed at length in chapter five.

Such use of form—a conscious, intellectual construct—can help keep us balanced as we try to navigate the often painful and scary images the unconscious has delivered to us via the dream.

Here is the poem:

St. Peter Said, "That's Good Enough," and He Walked Through

After my father died, he came to me
in a dream, and in a voice, raspy, some
where between a bad Brando and Bogey,
asked if I would accompany him

to the gate, talk him into heaven. It was
cold. March. And night. I didn't
want to go, could think of nothing to advance
his cause, but rose sulking and petulant

and followed him. Saint Peter, flustered, got
out of bed. Name one good thing, he said, waiting.
Finally I recalled the mutilated dog
he once shot to put out of its misery.

We stood there at the weatherless gate, still
strangers, odd pair out of sync until…

I noted earlier that I had thought my choice of the sonnet form for the exploration of this dream a random one. But the dream—and the poem—are always smarter than we are. Historically, the most prevalent use of the sonnet form has tended toward the love poem, which is what, without my knowing it, I had been writing all along to my father.

Sometimes what the dream leaves us haunted by is not so much an image but a phrase or line of dialogue. In one such dream I am talking on the phone to a young girl who, I think, holds me dear, who feels proud and honored to have me in her life. Though I cannot see her, I am aware of several things about her: she is about to become a teenager, she is intellectually challenged, and she is overweight. But, to my surprise and chagrin, she tells me she doesn't want to continue our relationship. When I awakened from the dream, her words explaining her decision—*You're boring, Cathy*—haunted me, again, for days. I knew I needed to explore that dream more deeply, especially the girl's mortifying words. My instincts told me the villanelle, a form that requires the alternating repetition of two lines, would require me to look closely at both the literal and the metaphorical meanings of those words. By the time I finished—or chose to abandon the poem—I was so startled by all my shadow stuff that had risen to the surface that I hesitate even now, dear reader, to share it with you. Be that as it may, here is the poem:

The Needy

You're boring, Cathy, said the girl in my dream.
I listened, surprised, from my end of the phone.
She was slow and overweight, about thirteen.

She was just being honest, not trying to be mean.
But I couldn't help feeling slightly dethroned.
You're boring, Cathy, said the girl in my dream.

I had been her mentor forever it seemed.
A program for kids from unstable homes.
She was slow, overweight, almost thirteen.

The sweetest thing once I had ever seen.
I bought her nice clothes, even a birthstone
Ring. I'm boring now, said this girl in my dream.

Her house was a shambles, but mine was clean.
Her mama a slattern, her daddy—plain gone.
She was slow. And overweight. About thirteen

years she'd lived in that mess. How demeaning!
I saved her! At least toss me a bone!
But *You're boring*, so says this girl in my dream,
slow and overweight, just turning thirteen.

The thing about this exploration that became more and more obvious to me as I kept repeating my two chosen lines was the level at which my righteous indignation continued to reveal itself. But what was I so righteously indignant about? The most obvious connection I made through my dialogue between the unconscious life of the dream and my conscious waking life was my fear concerning my beloved *little sister* Belen.

Belen and I had become matches in the Big Brothers/Big Sisters program when she was five years old. At the time of the dream, Belen was, indeed, about to turn thirteen. But I had no conscious idea of the inner dread and fear that was roiling inside of me. After all, I am a spiritually and emotionally evolved person. Right?

Crafting the dream into the villanelle brought to surface my repressed arrogance and misguided notion that our relationship was not about her and her needs but about my own insecurities and craving for affirmation.

Interestingly enough, though, Belen is not slow and she is not overweight. Neither does she live in a messy home with a *slattern* of a mother. This is where I will let you ponder the shameful hidden prejudices and biases (that had nothing to do with Belen) the dream was asking me to acknowledge and to rectify in my waking life.

But there's more. You'll notice that besides the alternating repetition of two rhyming lines, the villanelle also requires that the middle lines rhyme. As I continued to fumble around with the rhyme scheme of stanza two, I was surprised when the word *dethroned* drifted up into consciousness. Ah! Something else was happening in my life at the time of the dream: my three-year tenure as poet laureate of North Carolina would be ending soon—just before the turn of 2013. I would be relinquishing my laurel wreath to someone else. *Righteous indignation?* Hmm . . .

One of the most astonishing experiences I have had with crafting dreams into poetry revolved around a dream that was so surreal and messy and big and crazy that I knew I needed a form that, to me at least, also seemed surreal and messy and big and crazy; one that would at least give me something to start with and to hold onto as the images in the dream continued to buffet me around. That would be the sestina, a form that requires not the repetition of lines, but the repetition of six words that must appear in an intricate and varying pattern at the end of each of six six-line stanzas. The words must also appear in a three-line seventh stanza known as the *envoi*. Three of these words appear at the ends of those lines and the other three appear somewhere inside the lines.

Here is the dream:

I'm talking with my childhood-now-adult-friend Ruby about not wanting to go home. What she hates most, she tells me, are the slippers she has to polish for *them* (her aged parents) every day at five in the afternoon. My sister Rosi is somewhere out partying with Sissy Spacek. I need to go home but Ruby can't take me. She has a date. Someone lends me a car to drive myself home. It's very dark and my feet are cramped. I can barely maneuver the pedals. A few feet at a time is all I can go. The dream ends here.

The only rational connection I was aware of as soon as I awoke from the dream was the fact that Ruby's husband of three decades had recently died, followed—only two months later—by the unexpected death of my beloved younger sister Rosi. But what was to be made of those cramped feet and jammed up pedals, the slippers needing to be polished, all that talk of the dread of going home. And—really—Sissy Spacek?

My first step in crafting this dream into a sestina was to choose six words that had a lot of energy for me. I chose the words *Ruby, home, slippers, Rosi, Sissy Spacek,* and *feet.* In the first nine lines of the poem I simply retold the dream, ending the lines with my chosen six words. Because the words had to be repeated six more times, each time in varying order, I was forced to eventually move away from the images of the unconscious life of the dream into images from my conscious waking life. Here is where the dialogue between the conscious and the unconscious began. I give you my poem:

Ruminations on a Dream of Ruby and Rosi and Sissy Spacek

I'm talking with my friend Ruby
about not wanting to go home.
What she hates most, she tells me, are the slippers
she has to polish for them every day at five. My sister Rosi
is somewhere out partying with Sissy Spacek.
Someone lends me a car to drive myself home. But my feet

are cramped, cannot maneuver the pedals. A few feet
at a time is all I can go. It's dark, so dark, and Ruby
can't go with me, says she has a date. Somewhere out in Space—
that's where everything seems to be—home,
our mothers and fathers, dead for years. Now Rosi.
And waiting, always to be polished, those dreaded slippers.

My little town was excited when The Ruby Slipper
opened up. *A decent restaurant!* we all cried, though our feet
kept ghosting past until it closed. The kind of place Rosi
would have loved, and Ruby's
husband, too, were they not dead. *Gone home
to be with Jesus,* or so Ruby says. Remember Sissy Spacek

in that movie called *Carrie*? Spacek
plays a girl whose mind can send things flying—slippers,
and tiaras, tables, chairs, and saxophones, while at home
her mother's begging Jesus to save her daughter's soul, a feat
it takes a crucifix to accommodate. When Ruby's
husband died I drove five hours to be with her. The roses

I stopped along the road to buy were coral. Rosi
was too sick to travel with me. *Sissy*,
she'd phoned to say before I left, *tell Ruby
I'm sorry I couldn't come*. She, too, was slipping
away from us, though no one knew. My feet
ached during the funeral. Later at Ruby's house,

our shoes off, we talked past midnight of home.
The home we'd managed to escape. Then she rose,
led me to her old piano . . . her feet
and hands . . . the pedals and keys. Sisters.
Like sisters we had always been. *That* had never slipped
away. Though all else had, it seemed. Yet here, still, Ruby

and me. Soon they'll lower my sister Rosi
six feet too many down as I, too, begin to long for home,
begin groping all around for those ruby slippers.

As I struggled to repeat my six words—*Ruby, home, slippers,
Rosi, Sissy Spacek,* and *feet*—in whatever incarnations I could
conjure, I began to make surprising connections. The most
poignant for me was the fact that my eighteen-month-younger-
sister Rosi often referred to me as *Sissy*. Another was the
connection between the gas pedal and breaks of the car in my
dream and the real-life pedals of the piano Ruby and I sought
comfort in after her husband's funeral. Then there were the
real-life roses I bought for Ruby on the drive to her house and
the appearance of my sister Rosi in the dream.

But the connection of the dream's *slippers* and the real-life
closing down of my little town's The Ruby Slipper Café helped
me bring it all together. The dream is highly evocative—as with

The Wizard of Oz's Dorothy—of conflicting feelings toward home. Whether it is the literal earthly home for which we long— or whatever home, if any, awaits us in the afterlife—that longing is often accompanied by a deep sense of fear and dread. What comes to mind is the final scene of Liz Strout's Pulitzer Prize-winning novel *Olive Kitteredge*: "It baffles me, this world," Olive says, "I don't want to leave it yet."

Whether we begin with an abiding image or with a dream, we are setting up a dialogue between the conscious and the unconscious. And when we attempt to craft our dreams into poems, forms can be especially helpful in bringing order to the ostensible chaos of those dreams. Amazing, magical, mysterious things will happen. Minds will be expanded and enlightened, the human spirit, if only for a while, having come a little closer to that kingdom of heaven within.

ELEVEN

On Pilgrimage: The Work of the Writer

It took many years as a writer for me to realize that beginning a poem with a specific idea or some insight that the gods had somehow chosen to bestow upon me and me alone is the surest way to failure. But it would take teaching a weeklong poetry workshop in the Blue Ridge Mountains to disabuse me once and for all of that naïve—and narcissistic—misconception. Dog-paddling my way through a sea of Episcopalians at Kanuga's Summer Dream Conference, I would finally learn that the writing process requires a relinquishing of such control, a falling in love with the mystery that writing a poem entails. The greatest facilitator of my shift in perception was the canvas labyrinth spread beneath the basketball goal in the center's huge gymnasium, available, we had been told, twenty-four hours a day for meditative walks. The workshop I conducted each day met, by some odd hand of luck, in the small room adjoining that gymnasium.

During the morning session the first day of the conference, keynote speaker Alan Jones, then Dean of Grace Cathedral in San Francisco, made a statement that resonated powerfully for me: "Heaven is the place where you stand tall and straight and say 'I am.'" He then reminded us of C.S. Lewis's dictum: "In heaven we grow more and more real and substantial." Thinking Dean Jones's words might provide a nice transition into my poetry workshop, I asked the students later that day to give me five images—the *I am*s of memory—the colors, the textures, the smells, the sounds, the tastes that had shaped who they were. Then I shared with them my *silly* little exercise, discussed in Chapter Two, to help them call up those abiding images: *If my name were a color, it would be . . . if my name were a sound it would be . . . if my name were a smell, it would be . . . etc., etc.* As they worked quietly, I took the opportunity to venture from the room and into the gym to check out the labyrinth.

Lauren Artress, founder of the labyrinth project, and author of *Walking a Sacred Path*, had spoken that morning right after Dean Jones's presentation, her words still fresh in my mind as I walked out into the gym. Artress had explained that the revival of interest in the labyrinth was perhaps a result of the labyrinth's power to "utilize the imagination and the pattern-discerning part of our nature. The labyrinth," she said, "invites relationship and offers a whole way of seeing. When we allow ourselves to be whole, we allow new visions to emerge within us and within our cultures." As her words registered in my mind, it occurred to me that she could just as well have been talking about the writing process: *The power of the writing process lies in its ability to utilize the imagination and the power-discerning part of our nature. It invites relationship and offers a whole way of seeing. Writing allows ourselves to be whole, allows new visions to emerge within us and within our cultures.*

With these thoughts still echoing in my mind, I stepped gingerly onto the blue and white canvas replica of Chartres Cathedral's famed convolution of pathways, proceeding according to Artress's instructions given during her session: "Clear your mind and become aware of your breath. Allow yourself to find the pace your body wants." I was being a good girl. I was doing well, about to lapse, as I made my slow way along the path, into something akin to the writer's trance I experience when my writing is going well. It was then it happened. Another body, suddenly and head-on, had decided to encroach upon my space. My immediate assumption was that the short woman whose nose was now about three inches from my chest had somehow screwed up.

That evening I asked one of my colleagues if it was possible to meet someone head-on in the labyrinth. "Of course," he said, "if you're on your way in and they're on their way out."

"Oh," I said.

"What did you do?" he asked.

"I just turned and cut directly across the path and went back to my workshop students."

"Oh," he said, "so you jaywalked on the labyrinth."

I knew there were big lessons to be had from his jaywalking metaphor, but I was still feeling too indignant at that woman who had interrupted my reverie to be open to them.

If my name were a taste, it would be the taste of quinine my mother covered my thumb with to keep me from sucking it each night when I was four.
   —Valerie Tibbett, Sacramento, CA

If my name were a texture (touch), it would be cold and sticky like the juice of the watermelon I devoured each summer on the old picnic table at my grandmother's farm.
   —Salley Lesley, Chapin, SC

If my name were a smell, it would be the scent of the pine-knot fire, nights of the fox hunts my father used to take me on.
   —Barbara Ramsey, Stone Mountain, GA

If my name were a smell, it would be the smell of fear in our house as my mother held me, her shoulder tensing under her cotton blouse as her eyes darted elsewhere.
   —Jim Sones, Jackson, MS

I had returned to class—after my jaywalk across the labyrinth— to a room rich in the smells and sounds and tastes and colors and textures of a group of virtual strangers, of fellow travelers. And though we were walking at different paces, some of us just beginning our pilgrimage back to self, some of us already years into that journey, we all had one thing in common: we were, indeed, struggling, as Artress had said in her talk of the labyrinth, to know ourselves more deeply, to get back to that place in each of us where resides the divine, to find healing and peace, to temper and hone our gifts and to put them into action in the world.

And we were doing it with words.

On the second or third day of the poetry workshop, I told my students (for a reason I have now forgotten) the story of a little fourth grader named Marlon (as in Marlon *Brando* he had quickly informed me) who had stolen my heart the month before during a week-long residency at a summer writing camp in rural South Carolina.

I had been talking about the importance in poetry of grounding our emotions in the particular, the concrete. "There are no ideas except things," I quoted William Carlos Williams. And I had instructed these little people to think about a person they cared strongly about—that they had some deep emotional investment in—and then to think of an object they associated with that person. "Now," I said, "write about that object."

During my impassioned talk I had used the word *gratitude*. Soon after the students had begun writing, Marlon raised his hand and asked if he could use my word *gratitude*. "Marlon, Marlon, Marlon," I said. "That's not my word. I didn't make it up."

"Yeah," he said, "but I was afraid if I used it, you'd think I was copying you."

Then a tiny girl a few desks over spoke up in her stunningly clear little voice: "There's not enough words in the world," she said, "for everyone not to use the same word at least once."

There's not enough words in the world for everyone not to use the same word at least once. I was so taken with the simple brilliance of her statement that I asked her to repeat it so I could take it with me.

"Then, that's a quote?" another student asked.

"That's a quote," I said. The room grew suddenly quiet and everyone turned and looked at her for about nine seconds.

There was something Zen-like about her small insight. It certainly said something about what it means to be bound together in this big world, about the difficulty of expressing anything at all—our joy, our sorrow, our gratitude—when there are so few words and so many of us using them. I like to believe that when the lines and phrases and words of the poets I love—Dickinson, Hopkins, Donne—come sifting down again through my own voice that those poets are smiling through their now gumless teeth and tongueless jaws; smiling at the fact that not even for them had those words been enough.

It is amazing to me that the metaphor of the labyrinth has been a significant part of the spiritual world for so long. Though most of us associate it with the Middle Ages, the symbol of the labyrinth can be traced back at least four thousand years. Back to ancient Egypt, back to Crete, back to American Hopi Indians. During the Middle Ages, Christians and Muslims were expected to go on a pilgrimage at least once in their lives—Christians to Jerusalem or Rome and Muslims to Mecca. When the Crusades broke out, people couldn't make the journeys and so churches such as Chartres and Notre Dame created beautiful mosaic labyrinths on the floor of the church so people could simulate such a pilgrimage without leaving the safer landscape of their town or city. Many crawled the labyrinth on hands and knees to symbolize the physical hardship of making an actual pilgrimage.

We would learn during the week that there are no requirements, no prerequisites for walking the labyrinth. No degree programs needed before you start. No special uniform, no elaborate tools or texts. The labyrinth works for all creeds and denominations. People in wheelchairs or on crutches can walk the labyrinth. You don't need a workshop; you don't need a set of magic tricks to get you from beginning to end. You don't have to clean the house before you set out. You don't need to consult the experts for a set of rules to follow, for walking the labyrinth is like writing a poem or story: each journey must be taken according to its own set of rules. It is up to you to discover as you wind your way what those rules are.

I started class on Tuesday by having my students walk the labyrinth while meditating on the abiding image each had chosen to work with. "Let the image take you where it wants to go," I instructed, "even if the original abiding image morphs into other totally unexpected ones." So we stepped, each in turn, onto the labyrinth, our minds filled with pine-knot fires, a mother's darting eyes, the red juice of a watermelon, a quinine-covered thumb, etc., etc. And each in turn, we exited the labyrinth exactly where we had started, and went back to our little room to record the images and words that had arisen during our labyrinth walks. We sat quietly for the remainder of that day's time together, making our messes, creating our big-old-Michelangelo-inspired hunks of stone. We wrote into the mystery of our abiding images.

In the days before the ritual of pilgrimage became a symbolic walk on a mosaic labyrinth on the floor of the Cathedral, there were two holy destinations Christian travelers set out for. There was Rome where the Pope resided, and there was Jerusalem, the site of the events that had become the architecture of Christianity itself. But as a writer on a different kind of pilgrimage, I relate more to that boatload of Celts Dean Jones told us about one morning, who were spied tossing about haphazardly on the stormy waters near the shores of King Alfred's castle.

"Legend has it," Dean Jones said, "that the king instructed his guards to haul them all into the castle so he could interrogate them as to their whereabouts and their intentions."

I love the response King Alfred reportedly received from the leader of what must have been a wet and ragged crew of burly Irishmen: "We wanted," their leader answered the king respectfully, "we wanted for the love of God to be on pilgrimage—we care not where."

We wanted for the love of God to be on pilgrimage. We care not where.

I believe that as writers we must want, for no reason but the love of God, to be on pilgrimage and, like that boatload of Celts hauled into King Alfred's court, we must care not where. For with the work of the writer the ends and the means are of equal importance.

For the next three days, after having lived with their messes, their hunks of stone, my workshop students began, in Michelangelo fashion, to chisel and to cut away anything that was not the poem, then to shape and to polish and to release the poem that had begun as a single abiding image. And when they read their poems at the end of the week during the conference's grand finale, the looks on the faces of these much older, much more sophisticated poets, were just as victorious and pride-filled as the look on Michael Viglioni's face decades before when he discovered his little poem had, indeed, finally made it to the bulletin board at the back of our high school classroom.

Thumb

> She thought it wasn't right
> for a three-year-old
> to suck her thumb
> though my thumb was the only solace
> I remember in those early years.
> One night she gave me wine
> then covered my thumb
> with bitter quinine paste
> because her boyfriend was coming
> to visit and she wanted me out
> of the way. But in the middle
> of the night I got quietly up,
> washed the foul stuff
> from my thumb and stuck it
> right back in. I lay in bed
> awake in the room next to them
> sucking hard and long
> until it withered and wrinkled,
> the rhythm of my sucking
> putting myself to sleep.

> > Valerie Tibbett
> > Sacramento, CA
> > First Poem

Fox Hunt

What I remember most is the smell
of the pine-knot fire, its gray-white smoke
curling upward, making my eyes smart.

I felt so big sitting with those four men
as they talked of things of the day—then
started story-telling. Big Benjy who could spit

eight feet across a fire, or Willie
the hog-caller on the other side of Wolf River.
But mostly we would listen to the baying

of the hounds in chase—my father knew
the voice of each of his twenty-six hounds.
"That's old Loud on high C right now,"

he would say. Or "Little Lucy has taken
the lead." The Men would listen to the symphony
and figure the path of the chase

and where the fox and hounds might cross
the road. We would drive to that spot
in hopes of seeing the tired, panting

red fox in its race for life
followed closely by the hounds. Later
I was old enough to go hunting early

in the morning on horseback, enthralled,
at first, with the damp, earthly smell
of the swamp, the life teeming

in that primordial mass, until the men
began to shake the small wild
persimmon tree and the fox

fell into the midst of the jumping
hounds. I watched the tired dogs
drag themselves back to the fire—

some with bloody ears and feet—and flop
down ready to be petted. I had not
wanted it to end like this, imagined,

instead, each of us blowing
on the fox horns a baying symphony
of our own, calling the twenty-six home.

> Barbara Ramsey
> Norcross, GA
> First Poem

Adolescence

"My house," said Earl, "smelled
like coal-oil when I was growing up."
We sat, legs dangling
from the railroad bridge,
dropping rocks into the deep black pool below.

Earl's daddy's outgrown boots
were punching at the slag we dropped.

Down there concentric circles widened,
intersected, faded away.
We never talked serious, Earl and me, mostly sex,
which we never got, and cars.

Still, we hoped for both
and ached and ached and ached.
The license, it would come, but, oh, so slow.
The other . . . we felt ready for, pulse quickening

as we dreamed, though inwardly
the Adam's apple betrayed a silent gulp.
Long silences were common to our talks.

"Did your house have a smell when you was little?"
Earl asked me, as a blackbird
lifted from the wire below, winking
his red shoulder patch at us.
A mute memory was forming on my tongue, like a taste.

"Yeah," I said, "it was the smell of fear."
"Fear ain't got no smell," he laughed. "It's invisible."
I said, "It has no odor,"
but you know it when you smell it.
our neck hairs stand and hearing gets real sharp.
Even little bitty sounds are clear.
When I was a little towhead, I knew I knew that smell.
"What fear," he sneered, "could you have had
in that white picket-fence life of yours?"
I drew a blank:
I think I was too little to know,
but I could see it in my mother's eyes

and feel the way her shoulder
tensed under her cotton blouse
when she held me,
talking to me, her

eyes darting elsewhere. I dropped
another pebble, watched its slow
descent. "Can you," I wondered
to him aloud, "inherit fear?"

> Jim Sones
> Jackson, MI
> First Poem

Seed

That longed-for season here at last,
I'd run barefoot to the table
through the cool, tickly grass, yelling
"Me first, I want some!" Spitting

seeds, licking the sweet red juices
from my sticky chin, I wondered
if it was true, what they said
about the seeds. How if I swallowed one

a watermelon might grow in my belly,
worse yet, a baby. But it tasted, by now,
too good to stop. And so I ate
my fill, trying to decide: Better
with salt or without? Should I
use a knife, or risk getting its bright
red nectar all over my face and hands.
Then I'd rub my fingers over
its hard smooth skin
before throwing it away
not caring what it must feel like
stabbed and mutilated

at the bottom of that dark pail.

Salley Lesley
Chapin, SC
First Poem

When we have finished a walk on the labyrinth, we have traveled a distance of one-third mile. During this journey, we experience a casting off, a discarding, a letting go of the clutter of our lives. It is not always a pleasant experience, sometimes even painful and disconcerting—as in the beginning stages of a piece of writing. As we move closer to the center of the labyrinth, we become more open, expectant, empty, and receptive, less afraid of relinquishing control to the unconscious. Here we must allow ourselves to remain as long as necessary before beginning the move outward, the stage during which we begin to feel a sense of direction, order, wholeness and union—a sense of satisfaction at having completed the journey.

A member of a weekly writers workshop once asked me, "Cathy, do you think there's really hope for me?"

"What do you mean?" I asked.

"You know, do you think I have any talent?"

I was, momentarily, taken aback by the question. Was she asking if she would ever acquire fame and recognition? Would she get published? I didn't know how to answer her. I only knew that this person had written words that moved me deeply, had written poems that said in her unique voice something about the complexities of being human. She had written lovely, honest poems about her mother's death; poems, that had helped her through the grief and sadness of something that we all, eventually, must experience. So her question seemed a nonissue to me, and I felt a little ashamed when I remembered that I, too, had asked this same question twenty years ago to the leader of a conference workshop I was attending. What if on both occasions the answer returned had been "no"? Would we have gathered our humble efforts together and gone on about our lives, choosing a surer path? If so, then that's exactly what we should have done. Thank God that Pulitzer Prize-winning poet Maxine Kumin refused to listen when a teacher told her: "Say it with flowers, but for God's sake, don't try to write poetry."

Years ago in an issue of *Vanity Fair*, James Wolcott presented a scathing diatribe against the recent flourishing of creative nonfiction writing and creative writing programs and workshops. Consider both these quotes taken from his article:

> The proliferation of creative writing courses across the country hasn't expanded the audience for fiction, especially for short stories; if anything, there are probably more short-story writers in America now than short-story readers.

And later in the same article:

> In memoir writing, it's always the mother, Mom being the ultimate destination for a return to the birth of one's pain.

In context, these statements carry with them a sardonic, demeaning tone, as if both of these phenomena of the writing community have indeed greatly accelerated the rate of the decline of civilization as we know it. Perhaps I have merely lost sight of my own literary standards, but I see each of Wolcott's complaints as positives, not negatives.

First, perhaps the flourishing of creative writing workshops and programs hasn't expanded the audience for fiction. But neither does Wolcott's diatribe present any evidence that such programs have diminished the audience for fiction. Thus, what we have, unless my logic fails me, is the same number of readers and a great number more of writers. I fail to see how a growth in the number of writers could, in any way, be detrimental to the well being of our nation—not to mention the well being of every individual who musters the courage to tap fingers on keys, no matter the results.

And consider that second statement, Walcott's ostensible attempt to add insult to injury: "In memoir writing, it's always the mother, Mom being the ultimate destination for the return to the birth of one's pain." Insult? I think not. Simply another way of saying that our attempts through the writing process to turn our pain into art gets us ultimately closer to God. I do, however, offer my congratulations to Wolcott for realizing that the God this unsightly horde of writers is slouching toward is, indeed, a woman and not a man. My apologies, Mr. Wolcott. You've simply missed the point.

Unlike with a maze, it is impossible to get lost on the labyrinth. Faith will eventually get you to the center, closer to wholeness than you were before—closer to clarity. But like plowing through a piece of writing, any small obstacle might be all we're looking for as an excuse to turn and walk away—to jaywalk right across the page, to abandon the project completely once the trance is interrupted, once the writing begins to feel less than inspired. Who was it who said that anyone can begin a story or poem or essay or novel, but it takes a writer to finish one? As Dean Jones pointed out on our final morning, "We are a culture in love with answers, a culture that would be much better off to fall in love with questions again." For walking the labyrinth, along with the act of writing, must be an act of sheer faith.

When I departed the conference at the end of the week, I left with a cache of poems and vignettes composed by these homemakers, dental assistants, teachers, doctors, counselors, journalists, house painters, and ministers I would more than likely never see again. Our paths on our separate pilgrimages had converged for a short while and our love of words alone, our common struggle to express the inexpressible, had left each of us changed, a little closer to wholeness.

Heaven is truly a place where we can finally stand tall and say *I am.* "Where," as C.S. Lewis said, "we grow more and more real and substantial." I know no better way to attend to the spirit than to live the life of a writer. To be constantly on pilgrimage, or, if not on pilgrimage, walking a labyrinth of words. For it is the writer who, perhaps, after all, understands best Emily Dickinson's famous lines: "So instead of getting to Heaven, at last— / I'm going, all along."

Coda

If I have said anything in these pages that you, my fellow travelers, can use as inspiration and guidance in your own writing, reading, and teaching lives, then I have succeeded in spreading my *good news*. I can't imagine a better way of being fully awake in this world than to live the life of a poet. I want to leave you now, however, with a final poem, a kind of cautionary tale for anyone who might be asked to cast a critical eye upon the words of a burgeoning poet. Read it and take heed:

Syntax

Where haunts the ghost after the house
is gone? I once wrote. First line of my first
poem in my first creative writing class. I'd
been reading Byron, Keats, and Shelly, lots
of Poe, loved how the cadence of their words
fit the morass my life had fallen to. I had
stayed up all night, counting stressed
and unstressed syllables, my mother's
weeping through the door of her shut room
echoing the metrics of my worried words.
It was the year our family blew apart,
my mother, brothers and sisters and I fleeing
in the push-button Rambler with no reverse
an uncle had taught me to drive. I loved that poem,
finally knew how words the broken and bereft

could alchemize, couldn't wait to get to class,
could hear already in my mind that teacher's
praise. When it came my turn to read, the paper
trembled in my hand, my soft voice cracked,
years passed before I reached the final word,
before she took the glasses from her nose
and cocked her head. *You've skewed your syntax
up* was all she said. I remember nothing else
about her class. That spring her house burned
down, she died inside. *Where haunts the ghost
after the house is gone?* I had several alibis.

References

Brooks, Gwendolyn. "We Real Cool." Reprinted by consent of Brooks Permissions.

Collins, Billy. "Introduction to Poetry." *The Apple that Astonished Paris.* University of Arkansas Press, 1996.

Corey, Stephen and Warren Slesinger. *Spreading the Word: Editors on Poetry,* Revised & Expanded Edition. The Bench Press, 2001.

Duffy, Carol Ann. "Valentine" from *Mean Time* by Carol Ann Duffy. Published by Picador. Copyright © Carol Ann Duffy. Reproduced by permission of the author c/o Rogers, Coleridge & White Ltd., 20 Powis Mews, London W11 1JN

Flynn, Nick, "Bag of Mice" from *Some Ether.* Copyright © 2000 by Nick Flynn. Reprinted with the permission of The Permissions Company, LLC, on behalf of Graywolf Press, graywolfpress.org.

Frost, Robert. "Stopping by Woods on a Snowy Evening." *New Enlarged Anthology of Robert Frost's Poems.* Ed. Louis Untermeyer and Mary Silva Cosgrove. New York: Washington Square Press, 1971. 194.

Haden, Rev. Robert L. *Unopened Letters from God.* Haden Institute Publishing, 2010.

Hayden, Robert, "Those Winter Sundays" from *Collected Poems of Robert Hayden,* edited by Frederick Glaysher. Copyright ©1966 by Robert Hayden. Reprinted with the permission of Liveright Publishing Corporation.

Hopkins, Gerard Manley. "The Windhover." *Gerard Manly Hopkins: Poems and Prose.* Ed. W.H. Gardner. 1963. 30.

Hugo, Richard. *The Triggering Town.* New York: W.W. Norton and Company, 1979.

Lamott, Anne. *Bird by Bird.* New York: Anchor Books, 1995.

Mason, David and John Frederick Nims, eds. *Western Wind,* Fifth Edition. McGraw-Hill, 2006. 145-229.

Moore, Thomas. *Care of the Soul,* New York: Harper Collins. 1992.

Neruda, Pablo. "Ode to My Socks." *Neruda and Vallejo: Selected Poems.* Translated by Robert Bly. Boston: Beacon Press, 1993.

Pope, Alexander. *An Essay on Criticism* (Section 158). *Perrine's Sound and Sense: An Introduction to Poetry,* Ninth Edition. Perrine, Laurence. Harcourt Brace. 1997. 211.

Poulin, Alfred A. Jr. *Contemporary American Poetry*. Fifth Edition. Boston: Houghton Mifflin, 1991.

Smith, Dave. *A Few Sighs on the Subject of Editing, Etc.* Corey and Slesinger. 12-21.

Stocking, Marion. *Experience Through Language: On Philip Booth's Seventy*. Corey and Slesinger. 42-48.

Wright, James, "Saint Judas" from *Above the River: the Complete Poems* © 1990 by James Wright. Published by Wesleyan University Press and reprinted with permission.

Acknowledgments

Chapter Two: The authors of the lines from my "silly little exercise" are identified in Chapter Ten—*On Pilgrimage: the Work of the Writer.* Much gratitude to you all.

Chapter Eight: The earliest version of this chapter was written as the introduction to my third collection of poems *A Book of Minutes,* Iris Press, 2004. Thanks to Bob and Beto and Carmen Cumming for this and several other beautifully designed books.

Chapter Ten was originally composed as an oral presentation for the Charlotte Writers Club and a revised written version later appeared in *The Rose.*

Chapters Nine and Ten: I am grateful for the brilliance and humanity of these friends and colleagues whose books and presentations deeply informed the substance of these two chapters: Robert Haden, Alan Jones, Lauren Artress, Joyce Rockwood Hudson, Susan Sims Smith, Diana McKendree, Jerry Wright, Jeremy Taylor, Layne Racht, Bruce Baker, Stan Makacinas, and Alan Proctor.

I am also indebted to dear friends and fellow writers Karon Gleaton Luddy, Lee Stockdale, and Greg Lobas for reading and critiquing many of these chapters and helping me keep the faith as I brought this book together.

And to my editor Tom Lombardo who has been so instrumental in this process, I wanted to name him as my co-author, though he humbly declined the offer. And, of course, to Kevin Morgan Watson and Christopher Forrest who made it all come to fruition.

And always, more love and gratitude than I can express for my family—the entire gloriously disjointed kit-and-caboodle; my band of fellow outlaws known as The POETS; and Queens University of Charlotte's MFA faculty, staff, and students.

And to Christopher George Patrick Juett, the man who nurtured me in mind, body, and soul as I brought this book together. (Never mind that the saints his devout mother named him for have all since been disrobed.)

Cathy Smith Bowers served as North Carolina Poet Laureate from 2010 until 2012. She was educated at the University of South Carolina-Lancaster, Winthrop University, the University of Oxford, and the Haden Institute. Press 53 published *Like Shining from Shook Foil: Selected Poems*, drawing from her four previously published volumes and then brought together all four volumes in *The Collected Poems of Cathy Smith Bowers*. She served for many years as poet-in-residence at Queens University of Charlotte, and now teaches in the Queens low-residency MFA program and at The Haden Institute's Spiritual Direction Program and Dream Leadership Program.